Moonlight Crusade
Scott Kinkade

Special thanks to Cathy Lopez for once again powering through the drivel I write to make it not quite so drivel-y. Best editor ever!

1

Kyle struggled futilely against his chains. Locked up in the auto garage; held prisoner by a madman; abandoned by God; his friends murdered; constantly on the verge of puking; possibly no longer human; how could things get any worse?

The albino girl picked to watch him said nothing. She just sat there reading her trashy romance novel. She looked ridiculous in her red cult robe, but he could not laugh at these monsters. They had taken everything from him tonight, and he couldn't do a damn thing about it.

December 1. Twelve hours earlier.
The plane touched down with a thump before speeding down the LaGuardia runway. It came to a stop, the G-forces easing up on him. Kyle Falconer breathed a sigh of relief. "Whew! We made it." He could attest to being somewhat uncomfortable. Despite the winter weather outside, cold air from the

nozzle thingy above him hit with its cold breath. In addition, the plane was packed to the gills with humanity; not one seat sat unoccupied, and some of the people sported hefty girths. This was America, after all.

Next to him, Mike Miller stretched nonchalantly. "Of course we did. You think God would let us die when we're doing his will?" At six-three, Mike was a good six inches taller than Kyle. A well-built college football player, he was known as "The Oklahoma Tim Tebow." He might have been the only person still Tebowing, but that was to his credit.

Treia leaned over Kyle's seat from behind him. "I want to see the Statue of Liberty!" Her short, auburn hair hung down as she tilted her head down to address them.

"That's great," Kyle said. "But remember the real reason we're here."

Their branch of Campus Christians had come here, along with dozens of other branches, to attend the Empire State Christian Conference. Of course, that didn't mean they wouldn't get some sightseeing in.

The plane taxied up to the gate and, within minutes, people began disembarking. They all met up in the terminal in front of the gate.

Their leader for this trip was Tom Hill, a lanky, middle-aged African American with thinning hair but an undying passion for Christ. "All right, everyone. We have to pick up our luggage from Carousel Sixteen. Remember to be patient and give all the other passengers room to get their stuff off the belt. Now, come on—I'm Moses and I'm leading my people out of the terminal!" This elicited a light chuckle from the group.

After retrieving their luggage, they went up to the pickup area. The sky was a dreary gray. The bitter New York winter cold blasted them and they happily piled into shuttles that would take them to their hotel in Manhattan. Along the way, they passed through Queens. Kyle noted the rustic, humbled look of the place; there were probably great opportunities to minister here. The grandeur of Manhattan was nowhere to be found. And yet, there was a certain blue-collar appeal about it.

They soon passed over the Ed Koch Queensboro Bridge. Now, they could all see the magnificence of New York City. Towering buildings clustered closely together one after another; advertisements aplenty; food trucks/carts everywhere; countless theater productions. They drank it all in.

"Look at all those skyscrapers!" Treia marveled next to Kyle.

Sitting behind them, Tom said, "Actually, they aren't all skyscrapers. A skyscraper is made primarily of steel."

"Cool," Mike said. He sat next to Tom.

"We're now over Roosevelt Island," Tom said.

Their driver turned on the radio which had a news program going on. "There has been another series of killings in New York today. Attendees at a Maghrib prayer service at Islamic Devotion Society were brutally murdered during the service. Police describe the scene as a house of horrors. The Christian extremist group David's Purge has claimed responsibility. They've been calling for the annihilation of Muslims the world over.

"On the other end, the Islamic extremist group Ealim al'Ahlam, led by cleric Yousef Al-Bakir, has condemned the killings and promised a holy war if there are any more atrocities like this."

"How could anyone do that?" Treia said.

"I don't know," Kyle said sadly. "But I know one thing for sure: Those aren't real Christians. We'd never do such a thing. I'm getting sick at the very thought of it."

"It's horrible, but they'll soon be exposed for the frauds they are," Tom said. Despite his apparent confidence, there was a far-away look in his eyes.

"Stay positive, people," Mike added.

Kyle had to wonder at mankind's capacity for evil. Sometimes he secretly questioned why God kept them around. In such cases, he didn't hesitate to chastise himself. *You gotta have faith. Nothing happens without a reason. Even all this is the Father's plan.*

"In other news, the BBC recently reported another killing by the international assassin known only as *Le Faucon*—The Hawk. So named because of his precision and mobility, he killed his sixth high-profile target yesterday when he assassinated the Venezuelan ambassador to Great Britain in broad daylight."

The news report ended and Tom Paar's "St. Elmo's Fire" began playing. He sang about how his nemesis broke the boy in him, but they wouldn't break the man.

The shuttle eventually arrived at their hotel on Lexington Avenue. "Here we are," Tom said. "The Lexington Excelsior Hotel."

It wasn't a particularly large hotel, maybe ten stories. It had a plain brown façade like a lot of the buildings around here. However, the interior was another story.

"Whoa! A freaking fountain!" Mike exclaimed as they entered. Indeed, there was a two-story fountain in the lobby.

"It's beautiful," Treia said.

They checked in.

* * *

That evening, Kyle, Treia, and Mike sat on one of the beds in Kyle and Mike's room playing Trivial Pursuit: Bible Edition.

Kyle landed on yellow. Treia picked up the corresponding card and read it. "'To which tribe of Israel was Saul a part of?'"

"Too easy," Kyle said. "The tribe of Benjamin."

"Correct!" Treia said, high-fiving him.

Mike began singing to the tune of Queen's "Bohemian Rhapsody." "You're a show-off. Anyone can seeeeeeee."

Kyle sang back, "This ain't fantasy."

Treia burst into uncontrollable laughter.

When the game ended, they held hands on the bed and prayed. Treia led. "Our Heavenly Father, we thank you for bringing the three of us together in middle school. You have blessed us greatly and we are forever indebted to you. Please watch over us and those we love. We are yours. Forever and ever. Amen."

"Amen," Kyle and Mike said.

They got off the bed. "Guess I'll be heading back to my room," Treia said. She hugged them and left.

"We'd better turn in. It's getting late," Mike said.

"I'm with you on that one. It was a long flight from Oklahoma," Kyle said.

And, so, they went to bed. The conference wouldn't begin for a few days, but they had come early to do some sightseeing, and they would be getting up early.

God willing, of course.

✳ ✳ ✳

Kyle woke later that night. The clock on the nightstand read 2:15. Strangely, the door to the room was slightly ajar. Dim light from the hallway seeped in.

He got up and walked by Mike's bed to close the door. It was then he noticed Mike was gone. *Must've gone to get ice or something and didn't close the door all the way.*

However, his feet abruptly stepped in something warm. Turning on the lights, he discovered the floor was covered in a red liquid. Alarmed, he rushed outside. The lighting had mostly failed in the corridor. He headed straight to Tom's room, only to find his door was ajar, too. *Lord, please let everything be all right.*

"Tom!" he yelled as he rushed into the dark room. "I think something's happened to Mike!" There was a suffocating, putrid smell that struck him like a cannonball.

He hit the lights. Nothing could have prepared him for the sight awaiting him.

The mutilated bodies of his friends lay stacked in piles throughout the room. Some had limbs missing, some had eyes missing, and others could not be identified.

Treia and Mike were placed together on one of the beds. His throat had been ripped out. Her head was between his legs.

He almost screamed, but then something strange smelling was placed over his mouth and darkness overtook him.

2

Kyle opened his eyes, though not without a struggle. His head spun like a Tilt-A-Whirl. His stomach churned and raged.

He was on the floor of a long-since-abandoned auto garage. Carts with cobwebbed toolboxes lay here and there along with hydraulic lifts that allowed mechanics to see the undersides of vehicles.

A dozen figures stood around him, each of them hooded in red robes, save for the man in the center. Tall, bronzed, maybe six-six, he had long black hair and an equally black, trimmed beard. He looked to be in his forties. "So, boy," he said. "You believe in God?" He looked Middle Eastern and stood resolute with his arms to the side as he stared down at his victim. His teeth were sharp, like fangs.

A terrified Kyle noted with horror he was talking to him. Kyle didn't know what answer the man expected to hear, so he decided to be honest. "Y-Yes." He then added, "Please don't hurt me."

"Oh?" The man stared at him. "Won't God protect you?"

"Well... yes." But God hadn't protected any of the others, had he?

Kyle closed his eyes. *Oh, Heavenly Father, I know you're testing me, but* please, *let this be over quickly.*

The man continued. "Christians. The people who love the Bible are the people who don't understand it. It is not a book of love and compassion. It is a book of rage and oppression. 'For God so loved the world he gave his only begotten son.' But what everyone forgets is the amount of *carnage* he inflicted on anyone who committed even the slightest mistake in the Old Testament. Chloe!"

A much smaller figure to the man's left lethargically pulled back their hood to reveal a beautiful albino face. She looked to be no older than Kyle himself. Her white hair and pale complexion stood in stark contrast to the man's. "Yes... Lord... ungh... Kyrios," she said in a voice so quiet Kyle barely heard her. So, the psycho's name was Kyrios. That would be useful information if Kyle managed to get away and contact the police. And this Chloe was his accomplice. Still, it was small comfort now, and he doubted these people had been nice enough to grab his cell phone for him.

She handed Kyrios an intimately familiar book. "Let's see how loving God really is," he said and opened the Bible. "Exodus 20: verse 5: 'Thou shalt not bow down thyself to them, nor serve them: for I the Lord thy God am a jealous God, visiting the iniquity of the fathers upon the children unto the third and fourth generation of them that hate me.'

"Exodus 31: verse 14: 'Ye shall keep the sabbath therefore; for it is holy unto you: every one that defileth it shall surely be put to death: for whoever doeth any work therein, that soul shall be cut off from among his people.'

"1 Samuel 6: verse 19: 'He smote the men of Bethshemesh, because they had peered into the ark of the Lord, even he smote of the people fifty thousand and threescore and ten men: and the people lamented, because the Lord had smitten many of the people with a great slaughter.'

"1 Chronicles 13: verse 10: 'And the anger of the Lord was kindled against Uzza, and he smote him, because he put his hand to the ark: and there he died before God.'

"Ezekiel 24: verse 13: 'In thy filthiness is lewdness: because I have purged thee, and thou wast not purged, thou shalt not be purged from thy filthiness any more, till I have caused my fury to rest upon thee.'

"Hosea 13: verse 16: 'Samaria shall become desolate; for she hath rebelled against her God; they shall fall by the sword: their infants shall be dashed in pieces, and their women with child shall be ripped up.'"

On and on this went, with this madman—whom Kyle was now convinced was a cult leader—Listing every negative thing God had ever done. The Heavenly Father killed a bunch of people for questioning Moses. He allowed Satan to torture Job and kill his whole family. He essentially mind-controlled the Pharaoh into continually disobeying him so God would have an excuse to wreak havoc on Egypt. He wiped out Sodom and Gomorrah, and even Lot's wife, in a single night. He inflicted a plague upon Israel, killing 70,000 people. He let King Herod kill all those babies. And the list expanded with every verse Kyrios could find. And Kyrios could find a lot of them.

You didn't think about these things as a Christian. You brushed them off as God being God, doing what he has to do to keep the peace. God is just, Kyle always told himself. But when you were hit with all of them like a Biblical machine gun, it couldn't simply be brushed off.

"Stop!" Kyle said. Tears streamed forth, no vestige of self-control left. "You made your point! Just stop." God was good. God *had* to be good, or else there was nothing to live for. Kyle was breathing so hard, probably half the air in the garage was being sucked into his lungs.

"Made my point?" Kyrios calmly shut the book. "No. I haven't made my point. Not as long as there are still over two billion Christians in the world. In the grand scheme of things, I haven't even uttered a whisper. Everything I do is on too small a scale. But that will soon change. Chloe."

She advanced holding a syringe full of red liquid. "Hold him," Kyrios commanded.

Two of the other cult members grabbed Kyle and pulled up the sleeve on his left arm.

Chloe approached, her face a pale mask. Kyle panicked, tried to resist, but these guys had him in the tightest grip he could imagine. It might as well have been a mountain holding him for all he could do against it.

She examined his arm.

"Don't! Please!" Kyle yelled.

She stuck the needle in. There was a burning sensation as his veins lit up in a white light. A new consciousness assaulted his; someone seemed to be invading his head. He screamed and thrashed his head—the only part he could move. His lips drew back, undoubtedly exposing his teeth while threatening to peel right off his face. It was so horrible, in fact, he repeatedly bashed his head against the wall behind him to knock himself out, each slam intensifying the pain and darkening his vision.

Chloe casually grabbed his head to stop him. She stared at him with dead eyes. His stomach surrendered and he puked all over himself, the sickly beige-orange chunks splattering down his shirt and onto his lap. He barely noticed the pain of his teeth growing into fangs as that seemed inconsequential compared to everything else.

After an indeterminable amount of time passed, the voices in his head—along with the burning—subsided. He continued to suck in ragged breaths. He was too emotionally and physically spent to say anything.

Kyrios explained, "Chloe just injected you with my blood. I'm part of you now." This revelation caused Kyle to begin uncontrollably dry-heaving as there was nothing left inside him to dispose of. Kyrios then said to his followers, "Unchain him."

They did so. Kyle knew this was his chance, but what an absolute crappy chance it was. He was in no condition to make a run for it.

Kyrios dropped a dagger at Kyle's feet. "Pick it up."

"W-Why?"

"I need to illustrate a point to you." This man had not once smiled. His demeanor remained that of icy steel.

Kyle shook his head. "'Thou shalt not kill.'"

"If you don't, I'll kill you here and now."

A tortured Kyle agonized over his choices. He desperately wanted to avoid becoming a murderer like these people. But this seemed his only chance.

He reached with a trembling hand and picked up the dagger. His whole body shook uncontrollably while he stood up on shaky legs. He leveled the blade weakly at Kyrios.

"That's it," Kyrios said. "Come at me."

Kyle roared—*screamed* would probably have been a more accurate term—and lunged at Kyrios. However, he was abruptly overcome by an indescribable terror and dropped the dagger. He fell to his knees and cowered in a fetal position.

Kyrios said, "You understand now. You don't, but your body does. It recognizes me as a part of itself, like a limb. You can't kill me without being willing to cut off your own arm." It was then Kyle understood. These guys weren't human. For one thing, they exhibited too much strength for people of their respective sizes.

They effortlessly dragged him back and chained him up again. "What are you?" he said in a cracked voice.

"I call us *shahid*. You call us vampires. In the end, it makes no difference. Your kind has hunted *our* kind ever since the Crucifixion."

Vampires didn't exist. They were a fiction created by Bram Stoker. Weren't they?

As if reading his mind, Kyrios said, "We are much older than 1897." Neither he nor Chloe looked particularly old, but then, vampires didn't age, did they?

The horrifying truth dawned on Kyle. They had injected him with Kyrios' blood. That meant he was now a vampire as well. He shook his head as fresh tears streamed forth. "Why?"

"Why do all this, you mean? And why let you live? Simple. I'm building an army of anti-Christian soldiers. If I haven't already broken your faith, I will soon. You will join our cause, even if you reject us and fight separately."

The revelation of being manipulated in this way lit something inside Kyle. "God will destroy you."

Kyrios was unperturbed. "Open your eyes. God allowed me to do all this. We have operated without the slightest resistance from him."

He worked in mysterious ways. That was the reason, surely. He was biding his time, letting these maniacs get comfortable. And then he would strike.

"He let the Devil operate for a while. But even Satan will be defeated in the end. I'll never join you."

"Indeed, you shall. Even if don't participate in the coming war, God will not be able to count you among his followers.

"Rest up, Kyle. Your training is imminent."

The cult members all left the garage except for Chloe whose job it was to keep an eye on Kyle and keep him from escaping. She sat on the other side of the room reading a trashy romance novel, the kind with an impossibly-chiseled, shirtless man embracing a fiery redhead.

He decided maybe he could reason with her. "Listen, you don't have to help these guys. Just let me go, and I'll promise I'll try to get the court to have mercy on you." She didn't even look up, so engrossed was she in her book. "Please. You know this is wrong." Still no response. Kyle was getting frustrated. "Help me!"

"Quiet." Her voice was almost a whisper.

"What?"

Still staring at the pages, she said, "Reading. Busy. You're... noisy. Stop."

"Oh, well, I'm soooooo sorry," he said, his anger threatening to consume him. "Please forgive me for intruding on your precious reading time."

"You... understand. Good." She said it matter-of-factly and her expression never changed. Something was wrong with her mentally or perhaps emotionally. Maybe she was autistic? An autistic vampire? He had never heard of such a thing.

Reasoning with her wasn't going to work. His only hope was to get himself out of this. However, he was still chained up. Kyrios had said he was a vampire now, but Kyle didn't feel any preternatural strength or senses associated with being a member of the undead. He tried pulling on the chains quietly; he was afraid if he grunted, Chloe might hear him.

But, after about ten minutes of this, he gave up, exhausted.

"Chains... won't... ungh... break," Chloe said, still unwilling to take her eyes off her book. "Too... soon." Did that mean it would take time for his strength to increase?

"Any idea of how long that will take?" he asked sarcastically. She didn't respond.

Startlingly, the steel shutter next to him exploded inwards with a deafening scream. It flew at Chloe, slamming her against the wall. Kyle grimaced at the carnage; surely, no one could have survived that, and the albino girl had to be paste now.

In strode another cult member who proceeded to rip Kyle's chains apart like paper. "Let's go." It was a woman with a British accent. Why was one of Kyrios' followers helping him? It didn't matter. He had no choice but to obey considering the circumstances.

She led him outside. Snowflakes fell like silent, tiny paratroopers. Kyle's breath was visible in the cold. Across the street was a building with an LED sign that read "P.S. 76 The Magnet School of Health and Wellness."

"Where are we?" he said.

She replied, "Queens." She also had fangs.

Great. They were quite a distance from his hotel. He realized then with a sickening feeling he would rather die than go back there.

She led him down the street. It was a lower-middle-class neighborhood. He didn't know much about Queens, but he could tell they were not affluent here.

They eventually made it to the corner of 38th Avenue and 11th St. Many of the buildings he saw had been vandalized with graffiti. "Where are we going?"

"We need to get to Queensbridge Station. From there, we can get to my home."

"Why are you helping me?"

She said, "Kyrios and I have a difference of opinion. He thinks we should have bloodshed. I think we should have peace."

"But you killed that girl."

"Don't worry about her. It takes a lot more than that to kill one of us."

They continued southeast on 38th Avenue. "Is it true? Am I really... one of them?"

The answer crushed him like a safe falling on him from the top of the Empire State Building. "Yes. I'm sorry, but it's true. You are a vampire."

He was furious with her, his rage exploding into words. "Why couldn't you have gotten there sooner? If you had, this wouldn't have happened!" He knew she was his savior, but that didn't change the reality of the situation.

They turned right on 21st St and continued walking past a Shell station.

She responded cryptically. "This is an opportunity, Kyle. You will have the chance to shape the future. God's will be done."

"And where was God tonight?" he shouted. "My friends are dead, I'm a vampire, and..." His voice trailed off. It was too painful to speak anymore.

"You'll be able to rest soon. I promise."

They arrived at Queensbridge Station and descended the steps. The mysterious woman took off her cloak and exposed the black underside. She folded it and put it under her arm. Now, Kyle got a good look at her.

She was a little taller than him with long chestnut hair. She looked to be in her early forties, though no wrinkles were visible on her face. She had piercing emerald eyes. Astonishingly, she wore a pastor's pulpit gown. He still didn't know her name but was too emotionally and physically exhausted to ask any more questions.

They took the subway to Manhattan where they proceeded to walk to Greenwich Street. Kyle was about to drop dead, but his savior said cabs and ride-sharing services couldn't be trusted since some of the drivers worked for Kyrios.

Eventually, they came to a rundown church that clearly hadn't been used in years.

She pulled out a key and unlocked the door. They stepped into a dark narthex. Within moments, the lights came on, revealing a nave with two columns of pews. The stained-glass windows depicted various scenes from the life of Jesus: his birth, baptism, Last Supper, crucifixion, etc.

"Welcome to St. Rosemary's," the woman said.

Kyle staggered and collapsed into a back pew. He had expected it to be filthy, but it wasn't.

She continued. "We're near the World Trade Center Memorial. This building was abandoned after sustaining damage on 9/11. I bought it under a fake name and renovated it in secret."

"And just what *is* your name?" Kyle responded.

She came up behind him. "My name is Ursula Southeil. I'm not from around here, originally. I was born in Knaresborough in the UK, but that was a long time ago."

"Yeah, you're immortal, so I guess it would have to have been."

She hammered home another point. "You're immortal now, too, Kyle." It was too much. It was all too much for him to take in. Vampires? Immortality? His friends being butchered and propped up like grisly mannequins.

He shook violently and gave a heavy sigh. "I need to call my parents. Let them know I'm, well, not all right, but not dead, at least."

She shook her head. "That's a bad idea, Kyle. Kyrios has agents all over the country. He'll try to use your family to get to you."

A sudden spike of emotion gave him a burst of energy. "You can't be serious!"

"I *am* serious. If you want to keep them safe, you'll cut off all contact with them. I'm sorry, but that's the reality of the world you've just been dragged into."

He began sobbing. "This wasn't supposed to happen! God was supposed to look out for us! We're his children, aren't we?"

"Yes, we are. But our Father's role isn't to keep us safe at all times. It's to keep us strong. I know you don't feel like it now, but you will soon become stronger than you ever thought possible."

He let out a hysterical laugh. "I need some sleep. I'm losing my mind."

"I recommend only a few hours of sleep tonight so you won't be too rested in the morning. Don't forget: You're a vampire now. You can't be up during the day." He had hoped that part wasn't true. But his hopes, like everything else in his life, had turned against him tonight.

* * *

Angelica strolled through the terminal at LaGuardia. Her flight had arrived late from Rome only a few minutes ago.

To hide her profession, she wore a long, brown, breezy dress and black-rimmed glasses. Her dark-brown hair was pulled into a ponytail which came down to her shoulders. In addition, she carried a heavy steel case with ease.

She walked past a couple of security guards. Her enhanced senses enabled her to hear them whispering. "Hey, take a look at that woman."

"What about her?"

"She has special clearance. Didn't have to go through security."

"She some kind of government agent?"

"Yeah, but not *our* government. A little farther east."

She walked out of earshot. She didn't need to hear the rest. They could talk all they wanted as long as they didn't impede her mission.

After all, her job was everything to her.

3

Ursula gave Kyle a small office she had converted into a bedroom. It consisted mostly of a semi-comfortable bed and a desk. Like most rooms in the church, the windows were covered with steel shutters to prevent any sunlight from getting in. An antiquated lamp on the desk was on, bathing the room in a sickly light.

He currently lay on the bed, but he had missed his chance for sleep. Now, his brain was operating at full speed.

Why had God allowed this? Why hadn't he stamped out these monsters long ago? Sure, Ursula seemed nice, but the rest were, indeed, monsters.

He desperately tried to avoid closing his eyes, because when he did, he saw his butchered friends lying in that hotel room. He had heard about Post-Traumatic Stress Disorder. Now, he knew full well what it felt like. He couldn't stop thinking about it. Every gory detail assaulted him again and again, repeatedly coming around like a carousel of horrors. He was breathing rapidly, his heartbeat a ball bouncing between two surfaces only inches apart.

His friends were dead. He was a vampire. But the hardest thing of all was having to abandon his family. It crushed him beyond words. They were the rock on which his life was built. They had raised him with love and had introduced him to God's love as well. Ursula had promised him strength, but right now, he couldn't imagine ever being strong enough to cope with this.

His mind wandered to the Trivial Pursuit game earlier. He heard Mike's words as his friend sang to the tune of Queen, only this time, they twisted themselves into a cruel parody. *God is truly awful, anyone can seeeeee.* He instinctively tried to banish that thought, viewing it as heresy, but a part of him welcomed it. After all, God had allowed his life to be so thoroughly annihilated in the course of just a few hours.

But this wasn't unprecedented, was it? God had done the same with Job. Just said to the Devil, "Yeah, go ahead. Job's all yours." Maybe the Lord would replace Kyle's whole life when this was over. *So sorry, Kyle. Just had to prove a point to someone and you were just the lad to do it with.*

He managed to push the thought out of his mind, but it was replaced once again with the image of his dead friends, their body parts lying around, their blood choking the carpet.

He sat down on the bed and put his hands together to pray. *Dear God, I'm at the worst point in my life I've ever been. My life is over, and those monsters got me to doubt you. You're supposed to give us strength, but I didn't get any tonight. This has to be part of your plan, but to be honest, I can't see it. I need you now more than ever. Please, help me. Amen.*

The other shahid milled about, looking for clues as to where Kyle Falconer had gone. Chloe stood next to Kyrios in the abandoned garage as he held the steel shutter and examined it. This was Ursula's work. It had to be. By the time they had found out, it was too late to track them.

"Apologies. He... escaped," Chloe said. Her left arm hung limply; her body hadn't finished repairing itself yet. There was a gash across the top of her robe which extended from right arm to left shoulder also.

"It makes no difference," he replied. "No matter where he goes, he can't escape the fate I've set for him. By now, his faith is shattered. He saw firsthand what God will do to protect his children: nothing.

"I'm more concerned about our plans. Ursula has him now, and if they figure out what our agenda is, they may do something to oppose it."

Chloe remained silent. There was nothing she could add he did not already know. She would go along with anything he said anyway.

The shahid known as Mikhail came up to him. "Shouldn't we be more concerned with Guide? If they find out what we're up to, they'll sanction us," he said in his Russian accent.

"You all knew the risks when you decided to follow me," Kyrios said. And they had. Except for Chloe who was his slave and had no say in the matter. "All of us have been hurt by Christianity. That plague must be eradicated by any means necessary."

"Yes, but albino doll letting kid escape poses unnecessary risk." He stared icily at Chloe. She showed no reaction to this.

"You fail to see the potential of soldiers like Kyle Falconer. When faith is broken, it becomes just as strong going the other direction. He and others like him will come to fight against God with everything they have. And with the shahid strength I've given him, he will do much damage."

"If Guide doesn't find out and put a stop to it," Mikhail clarified.

"Do not question him." The petite Frenchwoman, Amalie, stood stern-faced behind Mikhail.

"I am simply saying we should not take on needless risk so close to operation."

"Enough," Kyrios said. "Everyone, fall in line."

All the shahid lined up in front of him with their arms behind their backs. The exception was Chloe who remained by his side.

He continued. "Chloe, what is our mutual goal? What is the one thing that binds us aside from the spoiled blood of Christ?"

Without hesitation, she said, grimly, "Annihilation."

"The rest of you," Kyrios said. "What do we exist to accomplish?"

"Death and rebirth," they said in unison.

He nodded, satisfied. "Good. Never forget our mission. All right, let's move out. We can't stay here now that Ursula knows our location."

* * *

December 2.

It was daytime. Not that Kyle could tell in his room in the church. His circadian rhythm was decimated on this new schedule. Ursula was sleeping in her room, but while exhausted, Kyle could not achieve this. He lay on his bed trying to shove away the relentless image of his dead friends.

The conference was in two days, but there was no way he could attend now. *Just try it. "Hey, I know I'm undead now and everyone else in my group has been butchered, but it's cool, I'm still the same on the inside."* He might be set ablaze just by entering.

23

He laughed hysterically. He didn't know why he found that funny aside from his growing insanity. He laughed and then burst into tears in the span of a second.

I can't live with this. It then occurred to him there was an easy way out: just run outside. The sun would obliterate him in short order.

Suicide is a sin. God would send him to Hell. His mood, having been relatively stabilized by the brief option to end his misery, was again crushed. But *was* there a god? He just didn't know anymore, though he found himself unwilling to take the risk. *How could Hell possibly be any worse than this?* He didn't know, but the Devil, if he existed, would find a way to make it so.

There was a phone on the desk. He picked it up and contemplated calling his parents. His hands shook; he wanted to call them but was terrified. What would he tell them? Surely, by now they had heard about what had happened at the hotel and had lost their minds with worry. He wanted to tell them he was... what? Not alive, as he was undead now. And decidedly not okay. The only thing he could say was he still existed.

That's a bad idea, Kyle. Kyrios has agents all over the country. He'll try to use your family to get to you. Ursula's words hung over his head like a cloud of absolute darkness. It was a risk he couldn't take no matter how much he wanted to. He missed his phone; he hadn't understood just how addicted to it he was until Ursula took it away.

Morbidly curious about the news coverage of the massacre, he turned on the TV hanging on the wall. It was a modern flatscreen, maybe thirty-two inches. A woman appeared onscreen with the headline "Mass Murder at NYC Hotel."

She reported, "New York citizens have been horrified by another mass killing, this time of Christians at Lexington Excelsior Hotel. A college group that had arrived in town for the Empire State Christian Conference was found brutally slain in their advisor's room. Neither police nor FBI are releasing many details out of respect for the victims and their families, but they have confirmed one student is missing and they hope to find him alive soon." The irony was not lost on Kyle. "Governor Masterson has declared a state of emergency in the city and has requested help from the National Guard. President Jericho has stated he will not bail out a poorly run Blue state and that they are on their own.

"In a follow-up to our previous story, the radical Christian group David's Purge released a video detailing their reasons for the killings at Islamic Devotion Society."

They cut to a close-up of a person wearing a bandana over their face. Only the eyes were visible. The pink eyes. Kyle noted the white eyelashes as well. "'We are hereby calling upon all our brothers and sisters to rid the world of non-believers. As it says in Deuteronomy 13: 'If your very own brother, or your son or daughter, or the wife you love, or your closest friend secretly entices you, saying, 'Let us go and worship other gods'—gods that neither you nor your ancestors have known, gods of the peoples around you, whether near or far, from one end of the land to the other—do not yield to them or listen to them. Show them no pity. Do not spare them or shield them. You must certainly put them to death. Your hand must be the first in putting them to death, and then the hands of all the people. Stone them to death, because they tried to turn you away from the Lord your God, who brought you out of Egypt, out of the land of slavery. Then all Israel will hear and be afraid, and no one among you will do such an evil thing again.'

"Muslims worship a false god. Therefore, we must show them no pity.'"

He had only been with her a short time, but her presence was already permanently burned into his brain.

It was Chloe.

* * *

Angelica stepped out of the elevator onto the eighth floor of the Lexington Excelsior Hotel. She was hit by the putrid smell of death. To her, it was the most familiar scent in the world.

An ashen-faced cop, who was standing directly to her right, turned to face her. "This area is off-limits and an active crime scene. Who are you?"

She flashed her badge. "Angelica Brassi, Special Crimes Unit of the Vatican. Fatima Protocol has been invoked. Under Special Treaty 789, you are hereby ordered to cooperate with me in this matter."

His face registered confusion. His eyes looked up and away, an obvious sign of trying to remember something. "Uh... yeah. I think I remember being told about that once. They said we weren't supposed to talk about it unless absolutely necessary. They threatened to fire us and revoke any pension we might have if we did. Real hush-hush, that stuff."

She put her badge away and smiled. "Believe me," she said, looking at his badge, "Detective Rourke, it has just become necessary."

He was perhaps just tall enough to be a cop, with a buzz cut of dark hair. "I guess if they let you in here, you must be the real deal. Never thought I'd get a Church bigshot. Suppose I should feel honored."

"You're pale, Detective. Is it that bad?" she asked.

He was visibly uncomfortable. "Worst anyone here's ever seen. Even worse than the synagogue murders, if you can believe that. We had to bring in every CSI we've got for this. Three of them couldn't take it and had to leave. Same with the maid who reported this to us; she won't be coming back any time soon. Matter of fact, I think there are more than a few openings now.

"There's no nice way to say it, so I'll just say it: It's a slaughterhouse in Room 809. The other rooms aren't as bad, just some blood, but 809 will give you nightmares."

"A nightmare in real life is simply an unfortunate situation," she said.

"Say that after you see it. Watch where you step."

She followed him down the hall. They carefully avoided CSIs taking blood samples. The smell became stronger the closer they got to 809. One of the downsides of enhanced senses was getting hit harder than normal people. Nevertheless, she had trained for this. She grit her teeth and soldiered on.

They soon arrived at a scene of indescribable horror. The CSIs had put several corpses in body bags, but numerous others still littered the scene. "What was the cause of death?" They stood in the doorway.

"Hard to say right now, but we haven't found any evidence of gunshots. Nobody heard any, anyway. Nor have we found any sharp or blunt objects that could have been used. By all appearances, it looks like they were ripped apart. But who would have the strength to do that? It's like a scene out of a monster movie."

You have no idea how right you are. "Did security cameras catch anything?"

He shook his head. "No, the lights went out briefly, so it was dark on this floor. The monsters must have carried this out during that time."

"Any fingerprints?"

"So far, no. But really, our problem isn't a lack of evidence, it's *too much* evidence. "This is... Oh, god."

He moved past her to the other side of the door where he wouldn't have to look.

She asked him, "So, in your opinion, could this have been done by humans?"

"Honestly? No. Like I said, this is a monster movie."

She continued to study the scene, connecting the dots in her head. "How many victims are there?"

"We believe sixteen. They were part of a college church group. We've locked down the hotel as I'm sure you noticed, but we can't account for the whereabouts of one member of the group. Kyle Falconer. We've found parts for everyone else, but not him."

Interesting. "Do you happen to have a picture of him?"

* * *

"Are you sure?" Ursula asked. Night had fallen and they had reconvened in front of the altar. They stood facing each other.

"Yeah. I could never forget her. She made a serious impression."

She pondered this for a moment. "If that's true, it means Kyrios is behind David's Purge."

"Does that mean he's also behind E.... Eel..."

"Ealim al'Ahlam. It's unlikely. For one thing, it's unnecessary. He only needs to control one side to instigate a war."

He groaned. "It sickens me to say this, but won't the killing of my church group cancel it out?"

"Perhaps temporarily," she said. "But if Kyrios finds a high-value Muslim target and kills him, all hope for peace would be lost. Never underestimate radical Islam."

"This is bad," Kyle said. "All he has to do is keep killing Muslims and taking credit for it. We obviously can't protect every single Muslim."

"No. Not the way we are now. That's why I must train you."

Huh? "Train me in what?"

"*Alraqsa,* the ancient art of vampiric combat."

Kyle sighed. "What's the point? I can't attack Kyrios without being willing to cut off my own limb, which I'm definitely not."

Ursula raised her index finger in an educating motion. "Not yet. But you can attack everyone else. The protection doesn't extend to them."

He shook his head. "I'm no fighter. I was raised to believe violence is wrong. Besides, those psychos probably have centuries of experience."

She replied, "Perhaps, but you have a mental edge."

"What do you mean?"

She waved a hand at him. "Look at yourself. You're a far cry from last night. Now, you're stable and composed. You're not thinking about suicide."

"How did you...?"

She smiled. "You're far from the first to go through this. Anyone in your position would be wishing for release. At any rate, you're smart enough to figure out what will happen if I don't train you."

He turned around and stared at the window depicting Jesus' crucifixion. "I'll be a sitting duck. And if anything happens to you, I'll be screwed."

"Yes," she said. "Which is why we must begin immediately. Sit down."

He did so in front of the altar while she turned off most of the lights, shrouding the room largely in darkness. "What exactly am I going to learn?"

"The Satanic Feats."

That was alarming. "The what?"

"Don't worry; that's just what the Catholic Church calls them. Remember: At the end of the day, they're merely tools. They can be used for good or evil. There are seven on them. However, I must warn you that the first one I'm going to teach you is rather unpleasant. That's why we're getting it out of the way now."

Gulp. That didn't sound scary at all. "What do I have to do?"

She sat down in front of him with her legs crossed. He mimicked her position. "This first one is called 'Thief in the Night.' It will enable you to disappear into the shadows. Close your eyes." He did so. "Regrettably, this skill requires a great deal of inner pain that most vampires carry due to the trauma of their turning. Think back."

"To what?"

"Last night. Remember what happened. Call upon as many details as possible."

Fear shot through him like high voltage. "What? No! I've been doing everything I can to avoid that!"

But she replied, "The nightmare won't end unless you confront it. Make the pain your own weapon to use against your enemies."

"I don't want to!"

"I'm sorry, Kyle, but you can't afford to be spared this. You must learn every Satanic Feat. But I *will* help you to direct your rage."

Despite what she was asking of him, his eyes remained closed. Maybe that meant something. He had to fight against instinct and summon the memory. He was shaking like crazy and having trouble controlling his breathing.

"What do you see?" she asked.

"My friends... Tom... they're..."

"You have to say it," Ursula said.

"They're dead! They killed them! I can see... Their blood is... God, it's all over the place!" The images were as fresh as they were last night and he had to fight back a sob. His anger rose in his throat.

"Who killed them, Kyle?"

"K-Kyrios. And Chloe. And all those other *monsters!*"

"Good," she replied. "Now, imagine the darkness this ordeal has plunged you into. Imagine the darkness surrounding Kyrios and his followers. Can you see it?"

"How could I not? They made it so *fucking obvious!*" He never swore, believing it unchristian. But he felt like he could break any rule now.

"Okay, now take that darkness and wrap it around you like a cloak." Like the physical cloaks of Kyrios and his bastards? "It's not your hell anymore; it's your weapon."

31

In his mind, he held a cloak of intangible darkness in front of him. With a flourish, he wrapped himself in it.

"Open your eyes," Ursula said.

He did so. "Everything looks the same."

She was smiling. "Ah, but it's not everything else we're trying to change. Look at *yourself*."

He held up his hands. The darkest black he had ever seen shrouded them. Like small black holes, they seem to consume all light. "Cool." He drank in the satisfaction of knowing he had taken one of their weapons for himself.

She stood up. "That's one down, Kyle. And, as I said, it's the hardest to learn. Emotionally, anyway."

"What do I look like?"

"Midnight, Kyle. You look like the darkest depth of night."

"Okay...? Umm, how do I go back to normal?" This was getting weird.

"You do that by doing the opposite of what you just did. You remember all the good things in your life. All the things you have to live for."

Sadness stabbed him again. "But I don't have anything like that now. They took all of it from me."

She went over to the light switches on the wall and flipped them, once again illuminating the room. Kyle's hands became fully visible again. "Fortunately, you can also banish it with literal light." He continued to sit there. "I'm sorry, Kyle. But you'll find your *raison d'être* again. Just give it time. God never closes a door without opening a window."

"Yeah, except it feels like God dropped the entire house on me."

She came back over to him. "It felt like that to Job. And to Moses. And to David. And to Christ.

And to Mary when he died. God drops a lot of houses."

Wasn't that the truth.

4

"The next Feat is called Devil's Reflex. Essentially, it's simply reacting with superhuman speed."

"Okay," Kyle said. "How does it work?"

She shrugged. "There's no trick to it. You'll simply spar with me until you learn it. Now, try to punch me."

If he had considered swearing to be unchristian, then hitting a woman was downright demonic. Still, he decided to go with it since he was pretty sure she could take care of herself. With that, he threw an awkward punch.

The next thing he knew, he was on the ground. In front of the altar. Ursula stood triumphant over him. "What happened?"

"I grabbed your wrist and flipped you."

"I didn't even see it!"

She smirked. "The Devil's Reflex allows us to move faster than any human. You have no experience using it, so you couldn't react." She helped him back to his feet. "Again."

He extended his arm in another punch while trying to focus on her attempt to grab him. However, a sharp pain abruptly rocked his chest. He doubled over, groaning. "What the...?"

She folded her arms. "I punched you in the heart. Not too hard, though. Alraqsa emphasizes strikes to the heart—the vampire's weakness. You must target it while deflecting attacks to yours."

"I thought you were just going to keep flipping me!"

She explained, "A large part of the Devil's Reflex is anticipating your opponent's actions. I can't train you to only guard against flips. Don't expect Kyrios or his family to be so considerate."

He managed to straighten up. "Family? Does that mean they *are* a cult?"

"Not as you know it. You see, most vampires belong to a family called a *manzil*. Each manzil is part of Dunia, or vampire civilization. I used to be a member of the Kyrios manzil. However, there are many others. The manzil who reign over the smaller ones are called the Guide. They're the leaders of Dunia, in effect."

"Does that mean I'll have to fight them as well?"

"I'm afraid I don't know the whole future. Some events are more fixed than others."

His eyes widened as he stared at her. "Wait, you can see the future?"

She gave a slight nod. "That's my Satanic Gift."

"Satanic Gift? What's that?"

"Every vampire gets a special ability that can only be utilized by them. Don't get your hopes up just yet; you're not ready. You have to master the other Feats first."

That was cool, but it presented a problem. "Does everyone in Kyrios' manzil have one?"

She shrugged. "Kyrios demanded secrecy within the group. Only he was allowed to know each member's Satanic Gift."

"What is his?"

"You've already seen it for yourself. No one he turns can attack him. He leaves a piece of himself in everyone whom he injects with his blood."

Interesting. It was somewhat of a relief as well. "You mean no other vampire has that power?"

"No. And even if they did, you've already been turned, so it wouldn't affect you."

He rubbed the back of his head. "Um... okay. Yeah."

"We've talked enough. Let's return to training whilst we still have moonlight."

* * *

After two hours, Kyle collapsed to the floor, exhausted. Ursula had thoroughly kicked his butt. However, he didn't think that was entirely the reason for his current state.

"What's wrong?" Ursula said while standing over him.

He was on his knees with his palms on the floor struggling to hold him up. "It's like the first time I gave blood." He probably wouldn't be doing that again anytime soon. "I feel sick."

"Ah," she said and bent down to put a hand on his shoulder. "Your metabolism finally resumed."

"What?"

"Didn't you notice you haven't eaten anything since being turned?"

"I..." He had been too focused on his agonizing situation. And... "I wasn't hungry."

She explained, "When you're turned, it's a great shock to your system. Your body copes by freezing its metabolism. But after a day or so, it resumes with a bang. Simply put, you need to eat."

A new kind of sickness came over him. Everybody knew what vampires sustained themselves with. "Please don't say it."

She did. "You need to consume blood."

"No, no, no, no, no, no, no! I can't do that! It's too much!"

She smiled. "I think movies and the telly have given you the wrong idea. Come with me."

Ursula led him downstairs to the dining hall. It was a plain white rectangle of a room with a small adjoining kitchen. She opened the fridge and removed a slab of white and pink wrapped in plastic. Kyle watched with fascinated dread as she put it on the countertop and unwrapped it. It appeared to be a raw cut of meat. Blood and all. Dear God, he was actually supposed to eat this, wasn't he?

He had expected some sort of bag or IV to drink blood from. "Won't it be hard separating the blood from everything else?"

"Not at all. Place your palm on it."

He did so, having no idea what was going to happen. The beef was cold and smooth with condensation still present. "What exactly is—?"

He lost his words when his palm attached to the meat with some sort of suction. His immediate reaction was to try and remove it.

"Don't fight it, Kyle."

Despite his apprehension, he managed to calm himself. He then noticed the blood on the beef was disappearing in the direction of his hand. More, importantly, though, his nausea was retreating swiftly. "Am I... sucking it up?"

"Yes," Ursula said. "An elegant approach, for a more civilized age."

What the...? "Did you just make a Star Wars reference?"

"I've been alive for centuries. Plenty of time to watch your popular films."

His hand abruptly detached from the beef. There wasn't a speck of red left on it now. "I don't taste anything."

She chuckled. "Of course not. You didn't use your mouth."

Kyle examined his palm, somewhat expecting to see a mouth or some sort of opening. But there was nothing. It looked completely normal.

Ursula explained, "The Feat is called Phantom Maw. It leaves no trace. A clean way to feed. By the way, you can still eat normal food. Your body simply filters out any nutrient that isn't blood and expels it as waste."

"And every vampire does it this way?"

"The refined ones, at least. Kyrios and his manzil still do it the old-fashioned way. However, they refuse to partake of Christian blood. You saw what they do with it instead."

Mike and Treia mutilated, their essence drenching the room. Now breathing heavily, he managed to banish the image. But it would be back. It would never leave for good. "I want to kill them and I hate myself for that. Christ said to turn the other cheek, but I can't do that with them. They need to feel the same pain as their victims. And yet, God wouldn't want me to do that."

He didn't know how Ursula would respond to that, but she still surprised him. "Most people don't understand him. Christians are taught that their god is a god of peace and love, but he condoned—and in many cases ordered—countless acts of violence."

"What do you think is his true nature?" Kyle asked.

"God is strong and proud. He rewards loyalty greatly but does not suffer disobedience. Of course, that's simply my own belief. Judaism holds the concept of *Shivim Panim L'Torah*—the 70 faces of the Torah. It teaches that God can mean different things to different people, and no one opinion about him is correct."

There was an obvious problem there. "Then, shouldn't he be the first to wipe out vampires?"

She said slyly, "Perhaps. But that would now include *you*. Many are victims who were turned against their will. Should they be punished for that?"

"I guess not. But nobody could possibly see Kyrios or his cult as victims. They're monsters, every one of them."

They began walking back to the sanctuary. "Most monsters were once victims, Kyle. A tragic incident or an abusive upbringing can shape anyone into a cold-blooded killer who knows only hate."

He decided to ask what had been on his mind for a while. "What made Kyrios into a monster?"

"That is not my story to tell. But his blood is in you now, so you'll find out soon on your own."

He didn't know what that meant, but it was clear she didn't want to discuss it, so he didn't pry any further. He did, however, continue to wonder about it as well as the other vampires with Kyrios. Like Chloe. What was her story? Why did she choose to serve him? He hadn't picked up on any malice from her—or much of any emotion for that matter. He just didn't know, and Ursula didn't seem entirely forthcoming.

They soon arrived back at the sanctuary. "I think that's enough for one night. Your skills are improving at an astounding rate. Tomorrow, we'll pick it up again."

December 3.

Angelica sat outside Café D'Alsace on 2nd Avenue on the corner of 88th Street near the East River the next day. It was on the ground floor of a modest, beige, five-story brick building with copious fire escapes.

The buildings in this area weren't particularly high like other parts of New York.

She had ordered caramelized butternut squash and mushroom risotto. As a dedicated vegetarian, she was still free to enjoy food such as this. The sky overhead was cloudy but otherwise, this was a fine day.

She put down her utensils as her phone vibrated on the table. She picked it up; she had received an encrypted message from the police who had been adequately cooperative thus far.

She ran the decryption program and received the following message:

RE: Person of Interest You Asked For

Video(s) Attached

She played the video. It had been taken from a subway station in Queens. It showed a handful of different people waiting for a train on a platform. None of them stood out except for perhaps a woman carrying a strange red robe. The young man standing next to her looked quite ordinary.

However, when he turned to look around, Angelica smiled. It was Kyle Falconer. As the video continued, they boarded the train.

Where was he headed?

Another attached video gave the answer. It showed Kyle and the mysterious woman exiting the subway not far from Greenwich Street.

The message had only provided the two videos, meaning if there were any others, they were as yet unavailable.

She looked at the timestamp on the first one. It was a few hours after everyone in Kyle's group had been butchered. He had somehow survived—or had been involved in the slayings—and now was with this mystery woman. Who was she, and how was she involved in all this? Perhaps she was the true mastermind of the killings and Kyle was her helpless thrall.

In any event, she needed to find them. There wasn't any more subway footage, so Angelica concluded they were still in Manhattan. However, Greenwich Street covered a lot of ground, and it would be difficult pinning them down without more leads. She had no idea how much time they had before the prophecy came true.

Her phone buzzed again, indicating another message. This one was from headquarters.

Supremo: *Rapporto sullo stato.* [Status Report.]

She typed her reply.

Angelus: *Sto progredendo costantemente. Finirò presto. La profezia sarà contrastata.* [I'm progressing steadily. I will finish soon. Prophecy will be thwarted.]

Supremo: *Non puoi fallire. Tutto dipende da questo. Sarà fatta la volontà di Dio.* [You must not fail. Everything depends on this. God's will be done.]

Angelus: *Essere in pace. Moriranno. Sarà fatta la volontà di Dio.* [Be at peace. They will die. God's will be done.]

She put the phone back in her pocket and began planning out the rest of the day. She would start by going to the subway station Kyle Falconer and that mystery woman had emerged from after leaving Queens. *Hmmm, not quite. First, I'll have the police meet me there and we can search together.*

Falconer would be found, and Angelica Brassi would have answers. Answers that would hopefully lead her to the rest of the killers.

And they would be stopped before they destroyed everything.

* * *

Kyrios studied a map of New York on his desk in an office of an abandoned warehouse in the city's Meatpacking District that night. This was crucial to their plan and every eventuality needed to be anticipated.

He was interrupted when Collins walked in. "Sorry ta bother you, but Ducane is here to see ya," the fair-haired Irishman said.

Kyrios had anticipated this. Their activities couldn't have gone unnoticed forever. "Send him in."

"I need *no one* to let me in," Ducane said as he came in on Collins' heels. He was impossible to miss as he towered over Collins' average frame.

"Leave us," Kyrios said to Collins who nodded sheepishly and obeyed.

Kyrios opted not to sit at his desk and instead to face Ducane as a man. The two were substantially similar in that they were imposing figures who had no room for humor in their lives.

"I'll get to the point," Ducane said. He was a member of the Septim manzil which was, in turn, a part of the Guide. But unlike Kyrios and his manzil, he wore a dark European suit which matched his slick, short, pitch-black hair. His chiseled jaw and rippling muscles intimidated most shahid, but

Kyrios had nothing left to fear. "Did you honestly think we wouldn't notice what you were doing?" he said in his baritone voice.

Kyrios was unphased. "We are shahid. We must feed."

"'Feed'?" Ducane spat out the word as if it were poison someone had given him as a joke. "Don't give me that *nonsense!* We are civilized. We laid out the rules for the lesser manzil to avoid being hunted by humans. You drain through the Phantom Maw and you don't kill."

Kyrios held his hands behind his back. "I believe the rule is, 'Don't kill unless necessary.'"

"There is nothing *necessary* about what you've been doing. The Church already hunts us, and you're going to expose us all to the rest of the world. I'm only going to say this once. Cease your actions at once."

"Very well," Kyrios said. "I shall reign my manzil in."

Ducane was silent for a moment—probably gauging Kyrios' honesty. Finally, "You had better. Any more mass killings and you will be sanctioned."

"You need not worry about that," Kyrios said, bowing.

Ducane grunted his acceptance. "I will report back to Claudius. He still worries about you." And with that, he lumbered out of the room. Kyrios was disgusted by his own deceit, but nothing could be done about it. He wasn't about to abandon his mission, but neither could the Guide be allowed to know that.

Collins returned to the room looking nervous. As a boy, he had been abused by high-handed Catholic authority figures along with his supposedly friendly priest. That had made him an ideal recruit. "Is everything all right?"

"Fine," Kyrios said.

Collins wasn't buying it. "He knows. Mikhail was right. Oh, god."

Kyrios got in his face. "God is the source of all our problems. Do not speak that name to me."

"But we're going to be sanctioned!"

Kyrios didn't move; he was an ice sculpture. "Of course. That was always the plan. You're a fool if you expected to cause World War Three and escape unscathed."

"I just..." Collins looked away, tension marring his features. "I just wanted to get rid of the Church. They ravaged my homeland. They need to pay. But the rest of us don't. We've *already* paid."

"And they *will* pay. But we must pay an additional price to make it happen. If you travel down this road with us, you must be prepared to sacrifice everything."

Collins turned his head back to look at him with despondent resignation. "Yes, sir."

* * *

Collins left the office and went downstairs. Most of the meat-packing stations had been removed long ago, but some equipment still hung from the ceiling. The remains of sawdust still clung to the floor in uneven clumps.

In the center of the floor, a sort of common area had been set up by the shahid. This consisted of two couches facing one another and flanked by chairs. His brethren lounged here. Chloe sat engrossed in one of her cheap romance novels. Collins didn't see Mikhail, though.

Someone tapped him on the shoulder. He turned around. Mikhail stood there with an index finger to his lips. Mikhail motioned for them to go to a more isolated corner of the room. When they arrived, he said, "Ducane saw Kyrios?"

"Yeah," Collins said, not wanting to talk about it.

"We are in trouble," the Russian said.

"Yeah." He didn't want to talk about it!

But Mikhail pressed on. "Some changes need to be made if we're to survive."

"What do you mean?"

"For starters, Kyle Falconer needs to be eliminated."

Collins was *not* hearing this. "Come on. Ya know Kyrios won't give the order to take him out."

A rare smile crossed Mikhail's lips. "Oh, but he will. Is where you come in."

Collins knew exactly what he was suggesting. "I could never do that. Kyrios values us, but no one is that forgiving. We'd be killed for sure."

Mikhail was adamant, though. "What do you think will happen if we go through with his plan? We will be sanctioned. You want to avoid, yes?"

"Of course. But the mission—"

"Will still be carried out. But Kyrios' methods are liability. I have plan that is much more discreet."

Collins spent several moments mulling it over. Then, "All right. But only because I don't want to be sanctioned."

5

"Absolutely not," Ursula said.

"Come on," Kyle pleaded. "I'm sick of being cooped up in here.

They stood in front of the altar. "It's too dangerous. People are looking for you. The kind of people you don't want finding you. Besides, where would you go?"

He shrugged. "I don't know. See some sites? I just want to get out for a little while."

She pointed an index finger at him. "I'm warning you—bad things will happen if you go out. End of discussion."

She left the room, presumably going back to her study at the other end of the church. Kyle sighed. He had been raised to respect authority figures and Ursula basically counted as one. She was his guide, his mentor, his guardian now. But he was twenty-one and could make his own decisions.

With that in mind, he went outside for the first time since arriving in that building. The cool night air and the mouth-watering smell from a nearby pizza joint greeted him. Despite the late hour, plenty of people milled about and traffic moved along like any other time of day, many of them hitting him with the heavy bass of their sound systems. This truly was the city that never slept. It occurred to him that the cold air no longer bothered him since his turning. He still felt it, but there was no longer discomfort.

Guilt crept in for disobeying Ursula, but he was committed now. The bigger problem was his complete unfamiliarity with this area.

He decided to just walk up the street in a straight line and see what was here. He set off and soon came to a stand selling T-Shirts. The Christian in him winced as he laid eyes upon one declaring "New Fucking York." *But are you still a Christian? Didn't Kyrios completely shatter every notion of a loving creator?* He didn't know. All he knew for sure was if God was real, he had allowed so many unimaginable horrors to happen. Why? Was his mind so alien his values could not be comprehended? Or were the lives of a relative few a worthy bargain for attaining whatever his unknowable goals were?

His friends butchered in that hotel room. Treia's head between Mike's legs.

He gritted his teeth and shook the thought from his head. He couldn't tell whether it was getting easier or harder to do. It seemed to be getting easier but the thoughts seemed to be coming more frequently.

He focused on the landscape in front of him. Block after block spread out like one of those mirror setups showing you reaching out to infinity.

He eventually found himself in front of a bar called Marvelous Mel's. The name was in neon baby blue letters above the door. There was a CCTV camera jutting out from below them.

He concluded now was the perfect time to have his first drink, so he went inside. He was greeted by a nice establishment. It was filled with nice furniture and even had a fake fireplace on the side opposite the entrance which was blowing orange luminescent strips instead of flames. The lighting was conservative and jazz music played softly overhead.

There was a fair number of people in the place; it was busy but not packed. He went to the right and parked himself at the bar, and the bartender, a young black woman with dreds, came over to him. "What'll it be, Sour Cream?"

"What?"

She smiled. "I'm just messing with you. You're pretty white even for a white guy." He supposed the vampirism *had* made him pale. "Anyway, I'm the owner of this little corner of New York."

He replied, "Oh, you're Mel?"

"Nah, I'm Jazmine. Mel's my girlfriend. I named this place after her."

Homosexuality is a sin. "Um... nice to meet you, Jazmine."

"Same here. Now, what can I get you?"

"Well..." he looked over the drink list on the counter in front of him. "What would you recommend for someone who's never had a drink before?"

"Oh, just joined the Booze Club, have we? In that case, I'll make you a Blitzed Reindeer. It's lighter than most of what I serve but you should still go easy on it."

"What's in it?"

"Red rum, peppermint, cola, and a candy cane."

Sounds good. "Okay, give me that."

"Just give me one second."

She began mixing the drink. It was then Kyle noticed the news broadcast on the TV above her. A male news anchor sat behind a desk in a studio. "The Grand Imam Abdul Batin Rabbani will be visiting New York to address the ongoing violence against Muslims in our city. Both American and Egyptian officials are being tight-lipped on just when he will get here to ensure his safety, but sources say it will be soon. Security teams on both sides are taking the possibility of violence as almost a certainty, and Ealim al'Ahlam's leader Yousef Al-Bakir has vowed to carry out a never-ending *jihad* if Rabbani is harmed."

He moved onto the next topic. "Police are still puzzled over the theft of two armored personnel carriers last week. The city's SWAT teams rely on them to infiltrate dangerous areas." A picture of a black behemoth appeared on the screen. The anchor continued talking about the theft, but Kyle wasn't interested.

"In other news, there was a press conference at the White House today, where President Jericho made his usual fiery remarks. We go now to Jennifer Jones live at the White House. Jennifer, what do you have for us?"

The scene cut to a newswoman standing in front of the famous building. It took her a moment to respond. "Rich, today, President Jericho renewed his call to place a hold on immigrants from what he described as 'hellholes.'"

The footage cut to William Jericho, an orange-haired hamster of a man in a suit, standing in front of a podium in the White House press room. "Folks, we're getting a bad deal. It's a very bad deal. Terrible, in fact. We need to say to Japan, 'We don't want you here.' They're bringing their kamikaze pilots, their ninjas, their tentacle perverts. Some of them, I understand, are good people. There are very good people on both sides."

"Both sides of what?" a reporter offscreen asked.

"Fake news, ladies and gentlemen!" Jericho said, gesturing to what Kyle guessed was the offending reporter. "Now, then. As I was about to say before I was so rudely interrupted. I have given the order to build a wall around the west coast, and we're going to make Japan pay for it. We'll take every last yen if we have to. We'll make them sell every hentai DVD they've got, but we'll make them pay for it." The audience was silent.

Jazmine put a red drink down in front of him. He took a tentative sip and his throat burned. "That's strong."

Jazmine shook her head. "How would you know? You've never drunk alcohol before."

"Good point."

She turned her attention to the press conference on the TV. "Now, there's a president we don't need."

"Yeah, he seems like a real nutjob," Kyle said. "I used to think he was all right back when he was just a real estate mogul. I even read his book, *The Science of Negotiation*. Now, I don't believe any of that crap."

She said, "Well, what *do* you believe?"

He put up his hands in an *I don't know* gesture. "I used to believe in a lot of things. God; conservatives; a certain amount of fairness in life. Now, I don't know."

"I hear you. I had a rough time years ago. I found myself a stranger in a strange land. But Mel, she saved me from that. Now, I have a purpose. You just need to find your Mel."

By now, he was buzzed and drinking more enthusiastically. "Well, I've got two women in my life right now. One's mysterious, and the other's a homicidal psychopath. There was another girl, but..."

* * *

He moaned and opened his eyes. He had a raging headache and no idea why.

Kyle looked around. He was on a ratty couch in an office somewhere. In front of him was a desk with file cabinets on either side of it. Someone was sitting in the chair at it. She turned her head to look at him.

"Awake, are we?" It was Jazmine.

He groaned and gingerly sat up. "What happened?"

"You started talking about a girl you knew. I'm guessing she's not around anymore. You started bawling and passed out. I brought you in here."

Oh, God. He remembered now. Ursula had been right; bad things had come of this little jaunt. "What time is it?"

"A little after five-thirty."

"AM?"

"That would be correct."

"Crap," he said. "I need to get back." Before the sun rose.

She helped him up. "You're right. We both need to get out of here pronto. I don't normally stay this long, but I didn't want to leave you."

A wave of... some positive emotion washed over him. He couldn't quite place it. "Thanks. I'm sorry I troubled you."

She smiled. "Don't worry about it. It's good to mix things up once in a while. Oh, the look on Mel's face when I get home. Priceless. Ah, but she'll probably be asleep when I arrive. Oh, well."

* * *

He limped back to the church, his brain seemingly stuck in a blender on "Max" setting. Panic started in

51

him when the first line of light blue appeared on the horizon, but fortunately, he made it.

Ursula was waiting for him while sitting on the back pew. She got up and came over to him, her face furrowed in a frown.

"I suppose you're pretty mad," he said.

To his surprise, she shook her head. "No. It was selfish of me to try and stop you. I was afraid for myself. It's a reminder that I must be prepared to face the road ahead."

"What does that mean?"

"You needn't worry about it. But tonight, we must continue your training."

December 4.

The Permanent Observer Mission of the Holy See, located at 25 East 39th Street, was both the Holy See and Angelica's base of operations in New York.

As she prepared to leave her quarters to continue her mission, her phone buzzed. She pulled it out to find a photo of Kyle Falconer standing beneath a camera somewhere. The accompanying message stated this had been captured outside a bar called Marvelous Mel's on Greenwich Street and the camera had shown him entering said bar.

Smiling, she put the phone back in her pocket. She hadn't been sure where she would go today, but now she had a destination.

She took a cab to Marvelous Mel's but found it closed. The plastic schedule on the door said it would open at 9:00 p.m. Very well. She would come back then.

* * *

Chloe sat on a couch in the common area of the meatpacking plant reading another romance novel that night. This was the fifth one this week. Kyrios kept her well-stocked.

Presently, the other shahid were out enjoying New York's nightlife. Crowds filled her with dread, so she always opted to stay home.

Because crowds meant death. People always died when Kyrios took her to a large group of them. But she never resisted him because she knew what would happen.

Footsteps echoed across the floor. Curious— no one was supposed to be here besides her. She looked up; Kyrios was approaching. Hadn't he left earlier to do reconnaissance for his jihad?

He stopped next to the couch. "Chloe. I have a new mission for you."

"Mission?" Inwardly, she shuddered. Her missions were usually the same, i.e., unspeakably bloody.

"I changed my mind. I need you to kill Kyle Falconer and Ursula Southeil."

She tilted her head inquisitively. Kyrios never changed his mind. "Kill?"

"Yes. Go out and find them. Don't come back until they are eliminated."

This was strange, but she didn't dare tell him no. "Understood."

"Leave at once," he said. "Our contacts in the NYPD said he was last seen entering a bar called Marvelous Mel's on Greenwich. If you're lucky, you'll find him tonight."

"Leaving... now," she said.

She had learned in recent years to internalize her vomiting.

* * *

After she left, he turned to the shadows in the corner. Mikhail emerged from them having used Thief in the Night to conceal himself. "Excellent acting," he said.

The façade of Kyrios melted away and there was only Collins now. "Sure hope so. But what are ya gonna do if she succeeds in killing them and reports back? Kyrios'll know what we did."

Mikhail had gone full smirk. "I have plan for dealing with her as well. And, afterward, we'll deal with Kyrios."

Collins was scared. He didn't know if Mikhail would stay true to his word. He might even sell the Irishman out. Nevertheless, his fear of the Guide was greater; Kyrios might kill him, but they would do much worse if the shahid's plan was carried out.

In all honestly, Collins didn't hate Christians nearly as much as the other shahid. He had been turned while still struggling with the aftermath of the abuse he suffered at the hands of the Catholic leadership in his church. But what Christians did to him was nothing compared to what they had done to the other members of his manzil.

Take Amelie, for example. During the Second Crusade, she had been living in the Rhineland. Unfortunately for her, she was Jewish, and a certain lunatic monk named Rudolf called for the extermination of the Jews. She was buried alive and was only saved by Kyrios who just happened to be passing through her village. He dug her up, but the damage was done. Amelie had a new purpose, and she was fully prepared to die for it. "And why not?"

she would later say. "They wanted me to die. Might as well give them what they want."

And she was just one example. Everyone in the manzil—aside from Chloe—had a horror story to tell involving their treatment at the hands of Christians. It wasn't that Collins and Mikhail didn't hate them; the two wanted to get their revenge *and* survive with their minds intact.

"I'm scared," Collins said.

"No need for that," Mikhail said. "All will be well."

Collins forced a smile, but he didn't share Mikhail's optimism.

6

Ursula countered Kyle's punch by deflecting it with her wrist, but that was becoming less frequent. He was getting in more and more hits.

As usual, they stood in front of the altar. Kyle was drenched in sweat while Ursula was as dry as a desert. "You're not just letting me get in hits, are you?"

She smiled. "That would be an insult to you. More importantly, you wouldn't survive if I did. Your enemies will do their best to take your life, so I must be as hard on you as I can. Your progress is due to your commitment and hard work."

"Okay, I'm glad—"

Ursula closed the distance between them and hit him in the chest with a palm strike. The result was a dull thud and Kyle falling flat on his back.

"Always be prepared for an attack," she said.

He said nothing as he had learned his lesson. Instead, he resumed the fighting stance she had taught him and moved toward her, wary of another surprise.

In one fluid movement, she pivoted towards him with a kick. "Kick" sounded too vulgar for what this move was, however. She arced her leg at him with the grace of a ballerina. He had spent the first hours of his training being transfixed by the beauty of it and getting hit, but he had learned that lesson as well.

He grabbed her leg and pushed it away. He knew she would smoothly transition into a kick with her other leg, but he jumped back and the toe of her foot missed his face by inches.

He continued to be amazed as her pastor's clothing didn't hinder her movements at all. "You fight like a ballerina. Where did you learn to do that?"

She relaxed her stance and stood straight. "Most vampires are taught the undead martial arts. Women adapt it to be more graceful. I don't expect you to perfectly replicate it. You must find what works for you, fighting-wise. And you've been doing exactly that in your time here. I should also mention that there are more Satanic Feats to learn, but we don't have time."

"Why not?"

She looked away. "We just don't."

Okay... "Well, you've already taught me a lot, so thanks."

She smiled. "It was my pleasure."

* * *

After she retired to her room, Kyle made his way over to Marvelous Mel's. The place was livelier tonight, probably because it was Saturday. Nevertheless, Kyle found an empty seat at the bar to the right of a pony-tailed brunette.

Jazmine came over to greet him. "Welcome back, Sour Cream. I wasn't sure I'd see you again. Kinda thought your first visit here would scare you off the bar scene."

"Not at all," he said. "I mean, yeah, it probably would if it were any other bar."

"Are you flirting with me? Because you should be aware of the stiff competition you face."

Kyle laughed. "No. I just... it's nice to have another friendly face to talk to." And another human.

"I think you mean, another *pretty* face to talk to."

Smiling, he replied, "I didn't see the point of buttering you up on account of the stiff competition I face."

"Touché," she said. "Now, what can I get you?"

The woman sitting to his left said, "I'd like to buy this gentleman an 'Unrepentant Sinner.'"

"Wise choice," Jazmine said. "Is that okay with you, Sour Cream?"

"Uh, sure. I'll be more careful this time."

Jazmine left to get the ingredients for the drink. Kyle turned to the mysterious stranger and said, "Thanks."

"Don't mention it." She spoke with an Italian accent and wore black-rimmed glasses. In addition, a slim black dress hugged her svelte body tightly. She was striking.

"Are you from New York?" he asked her.

She shook her head. "No. I'm not even from this country. I guess that makes us both strangers in a strange land."

"What do you mean?"

"You have the look of someone who no longer belongs in this world."

"You don't even know who I am."

The TV above the bar once again played the news. However, they abruptly cut into the broadcast with an "Urgent News" banner. A handsome, clean-cut anchor said, "We're breaking in here to report on a new story that occurred about twenty minutes ago. A car bomb just went off in London outside the London Waterloo rail station. Seven people are reported dead at this time, with twenty-four more wounded. They've all been taken to nearby St. Thomas' Hospital.

"We are being told the radical Islamist group Ealim al'Ahlam has claimed responsibility. Its leader, Yousef Al-Bakir, has issued a statement describing the attack as retaliation for anti-Muslim sentiment across the world."

"Jesus," Jazmine said. "All that for mere *sentiment.* Imagine what they'd do if something really bad happened."

It was terrifying to consider, and even easier to consider how Kyrios could take advantage of that.

"Did you hear about the mass murder that took place in the Lexington Excelsior Hotel a few days ago?" the stranger said. Kyle had momentarily forgotten about her.

Unfortunately, he had. "It was pretty... brutal, I hear." He didn't like where this was going, to say the least. His stomach tightened and his pulse shot up.

His friends' butchered bodies.

Jazmine came back and put down a dark concoction in front of him. "All yours, kid."

"Thanks, Jazmine," he said heavily.

Jazmine left to attend to other patrons and Kyle sipped from his glass. It had a bittersweet flavor.

"Oh, yes, it was brutal," the stranger continued. "Everyone was ripped apart. I would hate to have been a part of that."

He trembled and fought to control his own body. "So would I." He couldn't look her in the eyes, so he stared straight ahead.

"But one person from that college group remains unaccounted for. Now, I can understand running away from a dangerous location. But why not go to the police? Unless, of course, you had a hand in it, Kyle."

"Idon'tknowwhatyou'retalkingabout," he blurted out without thinking.

He then bolted to his feet. Realizing that only made him more suspicious, he beat down his rising panic and walked awkwardly to the men's room. He found it to be small—just two stalls and a urinal. It was, however, well-lit with a nice marble countertop that he stood in front of.

Who was that woman? Shit, she knows who I am. Ursula was right; I should have stayed in the church.

Okay, I need to sneak out of here and hope she doesn't follow me.

The door opened behind him and the strange woman entered. "You shouldn't be in here. This is the men's room," he said.

"Neither should you, Kyle. You should be dead after what happened. And you're *going to tell me* what happened." She locked the door.

He tried to get past her, but she grabbed his arm with superhuman strength and twisted it behind his back. Within a split second, she had him immobilized against the sink. He stared at the bizarre scene reflected in the mirror.

"You're lucky I have authority over this investigation," the woman said. "If I didn't, the police would swarm this place and take you away for questioning. As is, I want you alone so I can question you myself."

He struggled uselessly against her strength. "Are you a vampire?"

"I'll pretend I didn't hear that since you just answered one of my questions. Now, I'll ask another. Where are the rest of the monstrosities that killed your friends?"

"I don't know! They were in an auto garage in Queens, but I haven't seen them since I escaped."

"About that," she said. "How *did* you escape? Did that mysterious woman with you help you?" She meant Ursula.

These were legitimate questions, but Kyle didn't want to betray his savior. "I ran out when they weren't looking."

She scoffed. "As if vampires would be so careless. Who was the woman with you on the subway?"

He didn't answer. In response, she literally twisted his arm. A surge of pain shot through him.

"I-I ran into her *after* I escaped. I didn't know where I was and she showed me how to get out of there."

"Who is she? If she's just a local resident, you should have no problem telling me her name."

"J... Jennifer! Jennifer... Gantry."

She twisted his arm again, and he cried out. "Why the hesitation, Kyle? Surely, it would be easy to remember the name of the woman who saved your life. Now, then—"

Someone banged on the bathroom door. "What's going on in there?" It was Jazmine.

"Merda," his interrogator said under her breath. Then, to him, she said, "Don't make a sound."

The threat aside, he knew this was his chance to escape. "Help!"

"Bastardo," the woman said.

The door came open with a crash, splintering wood as it exploded free from the lock. In strolled Jazmine as if the door hadn't even been there. She locked eyes on the stranger.

His interrogator was caught off guard. Kyle planted both feet on the wall below the sink and shoved as hard as he could. Both he and his tormentor were propelled backward into Jazmine before she had a chance to regain her composure.

He ended up landing on his arm which the woman hadn't let go of because he landed on her as well. He howled in pain but managed to extricate himself from her. Wasting no more time, he charged out of the men's room.

"Wait!" the interrogator yelled. *Screw that.*

The sound of a scuffle behind him as he exited the room reached his ears. The crazy woman was probably trying to come after him, but Jazmine said, "Not so fast! You're paying for that door."

"Let go of me!"

Kyle swiftly left the bar. No doubt that heavy-handed woman would be coming after him. What to do?

Spotting a dark alley next to the building on the side where the church was, he had his answer. He dashed into it.

Angelica pursued Kyle Falconer outside. Not seeing him anywhere up and down the street, she reasoned he had gone into the alley, so she went wasted no time following him.

However, he was nowhere to be found. Nevertheless: "I know you're in here! You've been turned. That makes you my enemy. Next time I see you, I will kill you. Those were your friends, brothers and sisters in Christ, and you betrayed them by joining Satan's minions!"

He must have been using "Thief in the Night," but she couldn't see through that trick even with her enhanced senses. She had special equipment back at the Holy See that would do the job, but she hadn't brought it out of fear of being conspicuous. She hadn't known Kyle had been turned. She hadn't wanted to believe his innocence was taken.

It was a shame, but now he was officially an enemy of God, and no mercy could be granted such an entity. *Ti troverò di nuovo. I will find you again.*

✳ ✳ ✳

After the strange bespectacled woman left, so did Kyle Falconer in shadow form. No one had seen him enter the alley.

No one except Chloe. The scene Kyle had created upon leaving the bar had been noticed without any effort on her part.

A vampire could spot another vampire in shadow form if she knew he was there. And, unfortunately for him, she knew. She could kill him now, but she needed him to lead her to Ursula Southeil.

So, for the time being, she followed him.

✳ ✳ ✳

To: magicmistress1201@yahoo.com

From: mshipton@gmail.com

Subject: Farewell

This is to be my final message. Things have progressed faster than I originally envisioned, yet I must face my fate.

I met the boy I saw in my visions and I saved him from Kyrios and his manzil. He's going to do great things. My one regret is that I won't be around to guide him for much longer.

I want to express my eternal gratitude for everything you and the other girls have done for me. You took me in when everyone else wanted to kill me, so thank you for that. My life—or whatever you call a vampire's existence—was better for having known you.

With that, I will bid you adieu. May fortune forever shine on you.

Sincerely,
Ursula

P.S. In case you want to meet Kyle (the boy), you'll be able to find him at a bar up the street from here called Marvelous Mel's.

Ursula sent the e-mail and shut off her computer. Within moments, she heard the front door of the shut bang shut.

Kyle slammed the door and fumbled with the lock. His heart was practically an Olympic athlete with all the exercise it had been getting lately.

He stepped away from the door and stared at it, paranoid that crazy woman would burst through it. He didn't know if she was a vampire; she had seemed incensed at the mere suggestion. But if she wasn't, then how was she so strong? She had been asking him questions like a cop, but he had never heard of a cop like that.

"Kyle."

He jumped, spun around, and saw Ursula coming in from the left hallway. "It's just you," he said, both relieved and scared out of his mind.

"What happened?" she said. She was wearing a cream nightgown.

He told her. "Ah. I see. You met a Redeemer."

"What's that?" he asked.

She explained, "Vampire hunters working for the Vatican in Rome. They call themselves Redeemers because they believe they redeem unholy creatures through death."

That didn't quite make sense. "Wait, if she's not a vampire, why is she so strong?"

"The Vatican has advanced medical technology. They administer a procedure that grants super-human strength and enhanced senses at the cost of half the patient's remaining life."

He couldn't see his expression at that moment, but he imagined it was one of shock. "Why would anyone do that?"

"You might as well ask why anyone would slaughter a Christian college group. The answer is always hate. Push someone hard enough and nothing will be beyond their capability."

He looked down at the floor. "She said I betrayed my friends by becoming a vampire."

She put both hands on his shoulders in assurance and looked him in the eye. "That was not your choice, Kyle. That was Kyrios' choice and he will be made to answer for it one day."

Kyle collapsed onto a pew in an encore of his first night here. "I sure hope so. But, for now, shouldn't we, I don't know, get out of here? That Redeemer could find us here."

"That wouldn't be wise. They'll probably be combing the area for us. We need to stay inside where it's safe."

"You're right," he said. "In the meantime, I need some sleep *bad*."

Kyle Falconer had gone into the church. That must have been his base of operations with Ursula.

Standing outside, Chloe checked her watch. The sun would be rising soon. She doubted she would have time to kill them both and escape before that happened. Therefore, she decided to retreat to a nearby safe house and wait until tomorrow night.

Then she would complete her mission and return to Kyrios.

And wait for the next order to kill. Then the next. And the next.

7

December 5.

The shahid lined up in front of the common area in the meat-packing plant. However, there was one noticeable absence. "Where is Chloe?" Kyrios said.

"I haven't seen her since yesterday," Amelie said.

"Me, neither," Collins added.

"Not since last night," the Spaniard, Cortez, said.

Mikhail stepped forward. "I believe albino girl has fled."

"What makes you say that?" Kyrios asked.

Mikhail produced a piece of paper and handed it to him. It read:

You're evil. Can't take it anymore. Goodbye. Took your money.

Kyrios studied it for a moment without expression. Collins knew it was indeed Chloe's handwriting since he had copied her form when he wrote it—and thus her handwriting as well.

"A large portion of our funds *is* missing," Amelie said.

"Most unfortunate," Kyrios said at last. "We do not tolerate betrayal. Mikhail."

"Yes?"

"Find her and punish her."

"Punishment will be rendered," he confirmed.

"Good," Kyrios said. "Collins, you will accompany him."

"R-Right." This made him nervous. Why was *he* being sent? Did Kyrios suspect something?

Kyrios continued. "Now, then. The reason I have called this meeting is to announce we have uncovered the arrival time of the target. He will arrive in nine days at midnight. He will land at John F. Kennedy International Airport, where we will ambush and kill him. I will provide more details within the next few days. That is all."

* * *

Kyrios left the common area. Amelie followed him. When they left earshot, she said, "I see you've chosen to play along with their betrayal."

They were fools who had forgotten Chloe could communicate normally on paper. He replied, "Their doubts don't surprise me, even if their brazenness does. I trust it does not extend to the rest of the manzil?"

"No. The others believe in the cause. And Chloe, while not a true believer, wouldn't dare go against you. Even if it's only Collins impersonating you, she will obey."

Amelie's Satanic Gift was a potent weapon. Thus, she knew the moment Mikhail began plotting against them. She was his true right hand.

"Good," he said.

"But why let them try to kill the Falconer kid? Why not eliminate them before they can try anything?"

"This is a good test for him. He will become strong by facing them."

"Unless he dies," she pointed out.

"In which case, he was never suited to our needs. But I don't believe he will lose. Surely, you saw it: the fire in his eyes. He will burn brightly as an enemy of God."

"You mean, as an enemy of Christianity."

"It is all the same."

* * *

That night, Kyle was holed up in his room writing a letter to his family in the mail program on the computer.

I know you're all worried about me. There are so many things I need to tell you. It kills me to imagine what you would think of your son becoming a vampire. You were even more religious than me. Would you condemn me for something I couldn't prevent?

I love each of you just as much as before I was turned. I would call you, but I can't until this thing is settled. Rest assured; I'm being looked after. I was saved by this woman, Ursula. I don't know exactly what her deal is, but I trust her. She's been training me to take care of myself, although that hasn't stopped me from doing stupid things. I guess I still have a lot to learn.

Sis, I miss you most of all. I haven't even seen you since you left for your ecumenical work in Rome. You were always the most pious of us, a shining example for me to follow. I don't know if you would abandon me if you knew what's become of me, but the thought terrifies me. My hands tremble as I type this. If you forsook me, I wouldn't be able to live with that. I know suicide is a sin, but I have a feeling I'll have to commit some sins before this is over.

Your loving son/brother,
Kyle

He didn't press Send. He wanted to, but he was too scared. Scared of what could happen to his family.

And of what they would think if they discovered the truth. They stood as pillars of the Christian community. He thought back to the first Christmas he could remember. His parents had taken him and his sister to see a nativity scene outside the First Christian Church of Perry (their denomination). On the ride there, his father had recounted the birth of Jesus Christ in a manger. God had impregnated the virgin Mary with his son who would give his life to cleanse everyone of their sins. There was no room at the Bethlehem Holiday Inn, so they had to room with the animals. Three Wise Men showed up with gifts after having been guided by a star. Mary gave birth and all was right with the world.

Of course, that was the simplified version. Kyle wouldn't learn until college the Wise Men were actually Zoroastrianism priests called *Magi* (and might not have anything to do with the Bible version). Zoroastrianism was a whole other religion, which was probably why it didn't usually get mentioned when talking about the nativity.

Kyle had loved the story regardless of details. The whole idea of people coming together in peace and harmony always resonated with him. And his father had recounted it every single year, so regardless of what Kyle currently believed, the rest of his family remained diehard believers. Would they condemn him if they knew the truth?

* * *

Ursula prayed in front of the altar. Her prayers centered on Kyle and his immediate future. His trials truly began tonight. These past few days had been the easy part.

When finished, she opened her eyes. "You're right on time."

She turned around. The albino girl, Chloe, stood there, her hands crackling with blue energy. She had stopped mid-stride, probably by Ursula's words.

"Kill... you," she said. "Orders."

"I know," Ursula said. "You're the replacement, Chloe."

Confusion lined Chloe's face. "Replacement? What... means? Know... my... ungh... name?"

Ursula looked her over. "You poor thing. God has brought you here for a reason. I could explain, but you wouldn't understand. Not yet. Soon, though, you will."

The electricity in Chloe's hands intensified. "Enough! Die... now."

* * *

Kyle still stared at the email he had written but couldn't send. However, a sudden scream brought him out of it. His first thought was that the Redeemer had found them. Panic exploded through his body.

He rushed downstairs and found Chloe standing over the prone form of Ursula whose chest was riddled with holes, although he could see no weapon. In addition, smoke was emanating from them. Blood ran down his savior's mouth.

"Get away from her!"

Chloe began walking back toward the front door. She removed an index card from her pocket. "'Be up top,'" she said.

He rushed past her to Ursula and cradled her upper body in his arms. "Ursula." The word was of a higher octave than he'd intended, but his emotions ran wild.

Her chest was rising and falling with labored breaths. "It's okay, Kyle."

Anguish overtook him. "You knew! You knew this would happen if I went out. You said you didn't have time to teach me everything. This is what you meant, isn't it?"

She coughed and smoke came out of her mouth. "This is for the best, Kyle. What life could you have had with me as your only friend?"

"So, now I have *no* friends?"

She shook her head sluggishly. "No. You're going to make more. They'll be better for you than I ever was. They're out there waiting for you to bring them together. G-Good... bye... Kyle."

Her eyes went blank, and he was left with the crushing reality he had just lost another friend to vampires. He didn't fight the sobs; he let them come freely.

When he was done, he headed outside. That bitch would pay for this. *Murder is a sin.* Yes, and sins needed to be punished. She said to be up top, so that had to mean on top of the church.

He had never been on top of the church and didn't know how to get up there. However, he soon spotted a column of windows that went all the way up to the top on the front. The lowest one was too high for him to reach, so he decided he would just have to jump.

He took a running leap but was shocked by how high he actually went. He was a good halfway up the building when he reached it. He grabbed onto the outer edge of the window and managed to take hold, but he had a light grip and wasn't sure he could make it all the way to the top.

Then he remembered he had super-human strength, so he clenched his hands to get a deeper grip. Glass bit into his hands but he accepted the pain.

Deciding to throw caution to the wind, he bound wildly the rest of the way up the church. He felt like a gorilla or Spider-Man. He sunk his hands and feet into the wall to get foot- and hand-holds.

Before he knew it, he had reached the top. He scrambled to get onto it as he had run out of wall. He stumbled a bit, but he made it onto the roof.

He hadn't known just how big the church was until now. The roof spread out in front of him for at least three hundred feet. Unfortunately, he also hadn't known how hard it would be to fight on. There was basically a thin line of roof with the rest of it sloping sharply down either side. Now he understood why Chloe had decided to face him up here instead of down below.

She currently stood about fifty feet away, somehow perfectly balanced, staring up at the sky. She had discarded her red robe. Now she wore an oversized gray T-shirt and matching sweatpants.

"What's so interesting?" he said, his voice tinged with acidic malice.

"Beautiful," she said.

He followed her gaze. She was staring at the full moon. "You kill my only friend and still have the nerve to go sky-gazing?" he yelled.

"No... violence."

"What?"

"Moon. No... violence. No... killing. No... dying."

"You don't have the right to say that after *killing* Ursula."

She lowered her head to look at him. Tears streamed down her face. "Didn't... want to. Orders. Couldn't... disobey. Would be... ungh... one... killed."

"I won't go down so easily!" He was bluffing; he had no idea what she was capable of. He was also concerned about Ursula's wounds. Why had they been smoking?

As if to answer, Chloe raised her hands in front of her. Blue electricity began jolting into them, and within moments, knives of pure energy manifested. *That must be her Satanic Gift.* And he didn't have his yet.

She launched a lightning knife from each hand. They hurled toward him—probably at the speed of actual lightning. He only had a split-second to act.

His reflexes kicked in and he dropped to his stomach. The knives whizzed past him, crackling as they went.

He managed to get to his feet only to be startled by the boom of thunder. He fell to his knees. *That really is lightning!*

Chloe began running toward him, her feet seemingly dancing on the thin top of the roof. She was as graceful as Ursula. She raised her hand and flicked more knives at him.

In response, Kyle charged awkwardly and ran along the left slope of the roof. He managed to jump over the knives and they hit the roof resulting in a thunderous boom. Heat assaulted his body.

Fortunately, he was completely clear as he had jumped with everything he had. He sailed through the air and toward the back of the church. He was going to come down smoothly on it.

Or so he thought. But when he was a dozen or so feet away, he knew he would miss it and fall. His reflexes kicked in again and his body managed to contort itself in midair, turning around, his arms reaching back to the roof and precious solid matter.

His lower body went below the roof, but his arms managed to grab on. He pulled himself back up only to find a knife whizzing past his head. It grazed his right cheek, but that alone sent a torrent of searing pain through him. As a kid, he had once touched an electric fence on a dare. This was what it felt like but twice as bad. And he had only been grazed. He barely noticed the bang it made behind him.

He staggered and almost fell off the church, but his reflexes acted and he lurched, his palms coming down on the roof.

Kyle huffed, his adrenaline working overtime. This wasn't like his sparring sessions with Ursula. This time, his opponent seriously meant to kill him. He had thought Kyrios wanted to keep him alive for his satanic army, but it looked like the manzil head had changed his mind. He had obviously sent Chloe to do away with his enemies.

Speaking of which, where was she? He didn't see her anywhere.

A blue light above him gave him the answer: Chloe was in the air and diving at him fast. He scrambled forward, barely missing her. She came down with the utmost grace, swinging at him with an electric knife.

He had to fight back. He knew that. But it had never occurred to him he might be at a severe

75

disadvantage. After all, Chloe had her Satanic Gift and who knew how many years of experience. She had even managed to overcome Ursula without suffering a scratch. He had thought his righteousness would give him the power to win, but was he even in the right? He was trying to break one of the Ten Commandments; didn't that make him just as bad?

He found himself paralyzed with fear. This was the first time in his life someone was trying to take it.

But he would never win if he didn't actually attack her. He needed an opening.

A grunt behind him drew his attention. Chloe had stumbled upon falling and was now wobbling, trying to maintain her balance. *This is my chance!*

He came at her with his fist raised. However, in an instant, she stopped squirming and gracefully turned to face him. "Got... you."

She flicked a pair of knives at him. Still in mid-run, he couldn't dodge them. They slammed into his chest and sent indescribable pain shooting through him. He had never been set on fire, but he imagined this what was it felt like. He tried to scream but was paralyzed again, this time physically. He was somehow locked in place as the electricity seared him.

Chloe walked up to him. "Shouldn't... resisted. Would... have... ungh... made... quick." She raised her left hand which held four crackling knives. She positioned them between her fingers like Wolverine. "End... now."

You have to move! She's going to kill you if you don't!

She made a fist and pulled her left arm back in preparation to slam it—and the knives—into him.

In response, he roared with everything he had. Her left arm came at him.

He managed to partially break free of the paralysis. With his left hand, he grabbed her bare wrist. He did the same with his other hand and began sucking as hard as he could. Her eyes went wide; she realized what he was doing. "Stop!"

"Eff... you!" he managed to say.

Chloe struggled to get free of his grip, but the agonizing pain actually made his grip even stronger than it would normally have been. As it was, it had now become akin to a steel vice. She screamed—this was the most emotion he had seen her display.

He felt her blood coming into him. He was simultaneously repulsed and exhilarated.

But the acrid smell of smoke hit his nose and conveyed to him the roof was on fire. He needed to finish this before he was engulfed (although, he couldn't imagine that being much worse than the pain he was already in).

They continued to struggle. As the minutes went by, the smoke became more intense and the fire could be heard crackling along with the sound of wooden beams collapsing behind him. Kyle couldn't stop coughing and the carcinogenic air around him was overwhelming.

Eventually, Chloe's body went limp. Wasting no time, he shoved her off the roof. He had won, but there was no time to waste. The sound of sirens below doubled the urgency. Rescue crews would have questions he wasn't prepared to answer.

Thankfully, Chloe's blood had revitalized him. He took a flying leap onto the backyard of the church. He landed on a jungle gym, not that it broke his fall; they both crashed to the ground.

Picking himself up, he shoved the metal bars off himself and ran off into the distance. He had no idea where he was going; he only knew he couldn't stay here.

At least Ursula would be cremated.

8

Memories stirred within her mind.

She is playing all alone in the schoolyard. Rather, it is more accurate to say she is sitting by herself on the asphalt while everyone else plays.

Johnny Hacin and his chums come over to torment her again. "Look at the freak. White all over like an old hag."

"Go," she says. "Away."

"Freak can't even talk right. Her brain's busted," Freddie Solomon added.

Her brain works just fine. She can think clearly inside her head. It is only speech she finds difficult. She longs for a normal human relationship, but with guys like these giving her the royal shaft, that will probably never happen.

"Ain't that a bite," Billy Coen says, grinning.

"To her, maybe," Johnny replies. "To us, it's a big tickle." To her, he says, "You'll die an old maid."

She leaps to her feet and shoves him. He falls on his ass. His friends laugh. "No old!" she says. "Maid!"

She realizes what a mistake that had been when they set upon her. "Give the freak a shiner!" Johnny yelled.

She remembers the pain as their blows land on every part of her body they could reach. At eight years old, she has already decided the world is evil.

She leaps forward in time. This time, she is ten years old. Her father is a pastor and her mother is the choir leader in their church. They are as devout as anyone can be.

79

On this night, she is sitting with her parents watching Audrey Hepburn on the black box in their living room. She thinks Hepburn is the most beautiful and sophisticated woman on the planet.

Michael Clover, her father, sits beside her mother Anne on the couch. He won't let her watch anything sordid like Elvis "The Pelvis."

"You like Audrey, Chloe?"

"Yes," she says. "Audrey... good."

Anne whispers to Michael, "I'm worried about our daughter." Chloe still hears her.

"She gets good grades," is his rebuttal.

"The bullying is getting worse, and that awful school won't do anything about it. I'm thinking of writing a letter to the President."

He shook his head. "Eisenhower won't do anything. He's focused on the Reds. With Sputnik, they put one over on us. No, we just need to have faith that God will see us through all this." He then adds, "God isn't Red."

In her mind, she turns to look at them, but their faces are blank. It's been so long she no longer remembers what they looked like.

The power goes out. Her parents scream. A strange presence enters the room. A voice says calmly, "Hello, Mr. and Mrs. Clover. You've been making quite a name for yourselves in this town. Michael, you've been a vocal opponent of desegregation. You also said God hates homosexuals. And Anne, you've been supportive of all this." Chloe's heart is racing. She is filled with a sense of terror she doesn't understand.

The sounds of struggle reach Chloe's ears. "What do you want from us?" her dad says.

"I want two things. I want to punish Christians, and I want to recruit soldiers for my

cause. I've found it is more efficient to do both at once."

"What do you mean?" her mom asks.

He replies, "You two shall be punished, while your daughter will spend the rest of her life serving me."

Her father shouts, "God would never let that happen!"

"You studied the Bible, Mr. Clover. You know very well what God allows."

There is a ripping sound, followed by squishing. Something wet splashes her. Michael Clover screams. The sounds repeat themselves, only now it is her mother screaming. The last sounds she hears from her parents are moaning wails.

The man speaks again. "Tell me, child. What do you think of this world?" She realizes he is speaking to her.

She has long known the answer. "World... evil!"

"You will make a fine soldier." In her mind, she saw him smiling despite the total darkness.

Another voice says, "Are you going to turn girl now?" This man was Red.

"I will wait. An eight-year-old soldier would do me little good."

Yet another voice speaks, but this time, it's a woman with a French accent. Her father called them frogs. "Come, Chloe. We're going to make the world a better place."

Chloe doesn't believe her, but she has little choice in the matter.

* * *

She opened her eyes. She was lying on her back in an ambulance. An IV was inserted into her arm.

A paramedic stood over her. "Easy. You're going to be okay."

She was weak but still strong enough to get herself out of this situation. She ripped the IV out of her arm. "Hey, hey, hey!" the Paramedic said. "What are you doing?" In response, she sat up and rushed out of the vehicle.

Chloe was a few blocks from the church, only now it had been reduced a smoking pile of burning debris. She sped off after Kyle Falconer, the paramedic yelling for her to stop.

Kyle Falconer hadn't gone far. What he probably didn't know was when a vampire drank another vampire's blood, the latter temporarily gained the ability to track them.

He would be hunted down. But then what?

* * *

Kyle stopped several blocks away in a dark alley. The sounds of sirens blared in the distance. The pungent smell of exhaust from nearby cars reached his nose.

He considered himself to be shit out of luck. Ursula was gone. The church was effectively gone. He had nowhere to go. At least he had taken Chloe out before he got royally screwed.

He was surprised to find himself lamenting her death. He had become a killer. Was he any better than his enemies?

He was so caught up in his misery he didn't initially notice the figure sitting down next to him. When he did, shock exploded through him and he scrambled away.

It was Chloe.

"W-What are you doing?" he yelled, probably too loud for his own good.

She sat against the wall of the building behind them with her knees up to her chest. "Mission... failed. Can't... go... ungh... back."

He didn't bother to point out she could still try to kill him. He sensed the fight had gone out of her.

He sat down next to her. "Why do you follow Kyrios?" he asked her.

"Don't... want to. Afraid."

"Afraid of what he'll do to you if you refuse?" She nodded. "Did you mean what you said? About the moon being beautiful because there's no violence there?"

"Hate... violence. I... hurt." A tear streamed down her face.

He now had a better idea of this girl. "I thought you were a monster. But now I see you're the same as me. We've been dragged into an unimaginable situation by Kyrios."

"Kyrios... evil. Me... evil."

"I don't think that's true anymore. I think you're a victim just like everyone else whose lives Kyrios has destroyed."

"You are... kind. Thank... you."

Kyle inexplicably had the feeling he needed to protect her. It was the same feeling he had had towards Ursula. But why? He barely knew either of them, and Chloe had only just now stopped being his enemy.

"Thanks. But it looks like we're both screwed now. I have nowhere to go and you can't go back to the manzil. What do we do?"

"Safe... house," she said.

"Safe house?"

She nodded. "Can... go there."
He smiled. "Lead the way."

∗ ∗ ∗

She led him to an apartment building a few stops away on the subway. It was a tall brick building with restaurants and businesses next to the apartment part of it.

Chloe took him to the top floor and opened a door into one of the units. "Nice," he said.

It was an executive suite with space to spare. In the living room area, there was a couch and a TV was hanging on the wall. To the left of the TV near the door was a fancy mahogany desk with a computer and printer on it. The kitchen area had a huge fridge and all the appliances you would ever need.

But then Kyle noticed the windows. They looked normal. "Wait. What happens when the sun comes up?"

"UV... filter."

He exhaled. "That's a relief. I was scared there for a moment."

"Couch... there," she said, pointing to it. She then made her way to the bedroom.

Kyle wasted no time crashing on the ridiculously comfortable furniture.

∗ ∗ ∗

December 7.
He awoke later and sluggishly pulled himself off the couch. Exhaustion and soreness continued to tear at

him; he was nowhere near recovered from last night. The death of Ursula still weighed on him.

It was strange; he hadn't seen sunlight in several days and now it was appearing through the UV windows like no big deal.

His eyes spotted a sheet of paper on the keyboard in front of the computer. He picked it up and read it.

Hello, Kyle.

My brain doesn't allow for quality speech so I chose this method to introduce myself.

My name is Chloe Clover. For over 50 years, I served Kyrios out of fear. I can assure you, there was no love there and no loyalty. Terror kept me in line. I know that doesn't excuse the things I've done and I will have to bear my sins for the rest of my existence.

Without even realizing it, you convinced me to turn my back on the manzil. I realized it last night; you could have killed me but you didn't. Even though I murdered the person you were closest to, you spared me. I wasn't prepared to do the same. Not initially, at least. If you could find the strength to spare an enemy when your own life was in danger, I could as well.

I won't ask for your forgiveness. I know I don't deserve it. But please believe me when I say I'm not your enemy anymore.

I look forward to sharing more with you in the future.

Sincerely,
Chloe

Kyle studied the letter. He had, in fact, been trying to kill Chloe last night, although it was true, he made no further attempt to end her after she re-appeared in the alley. They were both spent in more ways than one at that point.

The creak of a door opening behind him caught his attention. Chloe came out wearing the same clothes from last night. "Read?"

"Yeah, I read. It was nice. I guess I should introduce myself, too. I'm Kyle Falconer. I'm from Oklahoma, though I was born in Texas."

She came over to him. "Nice... to meet. Kyle... Falconer." She smiled.

He smiled back. "Same here. But I think sharing our life stories can wait until later. We have more pressing concerns. What is Kyrios' plan?"

Her eyebrows furrowed as she seemed to focus on the words she needed to get out. "Grand... Imam."

"The Grand Imam Abdul Batin Rabbani? What about him?"

"Kill... him."

As far as evil plans went, that one was pretty effective. "If he kills the Grand Imam, there will be a holy war for sure. For crying out loud, they bombed that station in London just because they didn't like what people were saying."

"Yes. Countless... dead."

"How's he going to do it?"

"Compartmenta... lized," she said. "Only have... pieces."

He rubbed his chin thoughtfully. "So, no one person has the whole plan except for Kyrios. We have to stop him. But I don't think we can do it ourselves. We're pretty outnumbered."

"Allies."

"Yeah, we need help, but I hardly know anyone here. The only person who would be interested in stopping Kyrios is that Redeemer from the other night."

Her face lit up, and not in a good way. "Redeemer? Here?"

He explained, "One of them tracked me down a few days ago. She seems to think I was involved in... well, you know." He sighed.

His friends dismembered and soaking in blood.

Chloe began pacing around the room. "Redeemer... bad."

"Do you think there are more of them here than just her?"

She continued pacing. "Unknown. Work alone... sometimes. Others... groups."

"They might be willing to help us with this."

She stopped pacing and shook her head. "No. Sooner... kill us."

She had a point, but that limited their options even further. "Well, then, do you know anyone who could help us?"

"Not... many."

She headed back into the bedroom. "Where are you going?" he asked.

"Still... tired."

That made two of them.

* * *

"It's the damndest thing," the fire chief said as they stood in front of the church which was now smoking ruins. He had a distinct Brooklyn accent. "Eyewitnesses said they saw lightning, heard lightning. But meteorologists said there it was clear skies all night." The block had been cordoned off, naturally, although the media was doing their best to get in. They stretched and angled their cameras to get the best shots they could.

"I see," Angelica said. *Must be someone's Satanic Gift.* "Any bodies recovered?"

"Yeah, my boys recovered a middle-aged woman before the whole thing came crashing down. Damndest thing. Body was covered in burns consistent with lightning strikes. Again, clear skies. You want more information on the victim, Detective Rourke has it."

"Thank you, chief."

Angelica made her way over to a nearby police cruiser where Rourke was talking with another cop. A fresh-faced patrolman, by the look of him. When Rourke saw her coming, he said to the patrolman, "We'll talk more later." The third wheel left and Rourke said, "What can I do for you, Miss Vatican?"

His mood had improved tremendously since getting away from the hotel. "Well, for starters, you can lower your voice. My presence and identity are on a need-to-know basis."

"You got it."

"What information do you have on the victim?"

He replied, "Fingerprints identified her as forty-year-old Martha Shipton. She owned the building. Bought it right after September 11th."

"What other information have you uncovered?"

He shrugged. "That's pretty much it. We have the deed to the church and her birth certificate. Parents are listed on there, but we haven't found anything on them. We're currently working under the assumption 'Martha Shipton' is an alias."

"None of this adds up. Witnesses said they saw two people running around like *Crouching Tiger, Hidden Dragon* up top, a man and woman. But when we got here, we only found two women."

That piqued Angelica's interest. "I thought there was only one victim."

"Only one *deceased* victim," he clarified. "We found an albino girl in her early twenties, but she refused treatment and ran off."

"Tell me, Detective: Did either of them have fangs?"

"Well, now that you mention it, they did." He was getting visibly nervous as when she first met him.

"I trust you'll keep that out of any reports."

He shrugged again. "Not like anyone would believe any of this anyway."

Smiling, she said, "That is a healthy attitude, Detective. Make sure the fire chief knows that as well."

"Will do."

"There's just one more thing."
"What's that?"
"I'm going to need that body."

His business was killing, and business was good, he reflected as he reclined in his penthouse suite in a New York hotel. He picked up his phone and checked the balance on his offshore bank account. The influx of zeroes brought a smile to his face. The Russian had held up his end of the deal. Now, all that was left was for the killer to honor his.

9

0 A.D.

They stared up at the broken man in front of them on Golgotha. It had been a long day for everyone involved, and the sun had only just now begun to set. "So much for the King of the Jews," Claudius said.

"But they say he performed miracles," Longinus said. Like Claudius, he was a Roman soldier. Everyone had left except for the two of them. It would be their job to get the man down from the cross. "He had powers."

"And still he died."

But Longinus wasn't convinced. He continued to stare at the man called Christ atop Calgary. "Is he truly dead? Let us find out."

He took his spear and pierced the side of Christ. A mixture of blood and water oozed out. Longinus pulled the spear's head up to his face. The blood on it was glowing a faint orange. It pulsated with unknowable energy.

"What is it?" Claudius said.

Longinus stared at it, entranced. "Power."

"So? What can be done with it now?"

Longinus grinned like a hungry wolf. "The blood was in him. We need to put it in *us*."

"You are mad."

Longinus didn't seem to be listening. He stuck out his tongue and licked the glowing blood off the spear head. Claudius recoiled at this and took a step away from Longinus.

Longinus stood there a moment, waiting for something to happen. He wasn't disappointed. His body exploded in convulsions. He roared as that same glow came over his entire body.

After a few moments, he calmed down. "I feel it! I am stronger now than I have ever been!" He flexed his muscles and growled.

"Truly?" Claudius said, astonished.

"You must have a taste yourself! Join me in this!"

Longinus held out the spear to Claudius who stared at it. He was intrigued yet still suspicious. Finally, he decided to throw caution to the wind and do it. He licked the remaining blood and swallowed it. It had a copper taste same as normal blood, though it felt alive in his mouth. He couldn't explain it.

The pain arrived with the force of an entire legion. It was even more excruciating than Longinus had made it look. His body was wracked by spasms and it contorted viciously. Soon, though, it subsided.

A feeling of strength and virility soared through his body. He had never in his life felt this powerful. He firmly believed he could defeat any of the Legion's best warriors in combat. "It is true!" he declared. "The King of the Jews was special indeed."

"Should we share this with our brothers?"

Claudius laughed. "Why give up our newfound advantage? Let them wonder at our strength!"

"Agreed."

Claudius then noticed the increased brightness outside. "I thought the sun had set already."

"It has. It is below the horizon."

"Then, why is it so bright out?"

Longinus looked around, a mildly concerned look on his face. "I do not know. But has it also gotten hotter out here?"

"Indeed, it has!"

Within moments, Claudius' exposed skin began burning. He slapped at it to put out the tiny fires forming.

"We must seek shelter!" Longinus said.

They fled to a nearby cave. "Damn you, Longinus!" Claudius yelled when they were safely inside. "What have we done?"

They stood facing one another in the dark yet able to see clearly. His fellow soldier replied grimly, "We gained power, but an unforeseen cost."

Claudius was in anguish now. "That man Christ was able to walk in sunlight. Why can we not?"

Longinus could only speculate. "He was dead. The blood must have gone bad."

"Are we doomed to stay in the shadows for the rest of our lives?"

Longinus shouted, "I do not have the answers you seek! I seek them as well but do not have them."

Claudius became aware of a gnawing ravenousness in his stomach. "I am hungry."

"As am I. We did work hard today, after all."

But that wasn't what concerned Claudius. He now found Longinus... appetizing.

Both of them breathed heavily and shook with their growing hunger. It was a madness that threatened to consume them. Both began growling animalistically.

Claudius was vaguely aware of setting upon his friend in a bestial frenzy.

* * *

July 15, 1099 A.D.

Night had fallen, but the battle continued. The defender had cut down dozens of Christian knights but there was no end to them. They were determined to take Jerusalem and it seemed Allah was not on the side of the Muslim faithful this night.

There was chaos in the streets as defenders clashed with the invaders, both sides mustering all the ferocity of tigers. Sadly, the invaders weren't content to merely kill the defenders; everywhere, they were turning their blades and arrows against the helpless citizens. They wanted to wipe the city—and probably the entire Holy Land—of the so-called pagan scourge.

One man knew the truth. The battle was lost. His only desire was to get his family out of the sea of stone that was Jerusalem. They had taken shelter in the Dome of the Rock and he was running there as fast as he could. He pumped his legs relentlessly, fighting for every step he took toward his destination. His chest ached with the need to rest his heavy breathing. He only stopped when he was challenged by an invader, and even then, it was only long enough to put his foe to the sword.

He raced past a *souk*. The marketplace was burning, and all manner of wares set alight, their respective owners fighting to put them out. The choking smell assailed him. Countless people screamed and wailed from all parts of the city.

He made his way north along the Western Wall and soon arrived at the steps leading up to the Dome of the Rock. To his horror, he found them guarded by four Crusaders, the red crosses on their chests mocking his own faith. "Stand aside, you filthy mongrels!" he yelled in Arabic. They replied in their own language—which he did not understand—and came down the steps, their swords drawn.

The first Crusader to reach him came down with a kick to knock him off the steps. However, he deftly sidestepped it; Crusader armor was heavy and their helmet was difficult to breathe in, which slowed them down. He, on the other hand, wore no armor at the moment.

He swung his heavy sword into the enemy's head, causing him to stumble and lose his helmet. He went down and did not get back up.

The other three Crusaders, having seen the fate of their friend, slowed their approach. They then spread out to surround him on the steps. He swung at the man directly in front of him. The man blocked his attack but was staggered. The Muslim responded by reaching into his pocket and pulled out several needles which he hurled into the occularium—the narrow slit in the Crusader helmet which allowed him to see—penetrating his eyes. The man howled in pain and the defender shoved past him.

He ran up the steps and into the large courtyard that housed the Dome of the Rock. He veered right after leaving the view of the Crusaders. The two remaining ones hurried after him, but that was part of his plan. As soon as they appeared at the top of the steps, he swung his sword with all his might across both their chests. Caught off guard, they went down the steps, knocked over the blinded Crusader, and crumpled in a heap at the bottom.

With them out of the way, he hurried towards the Dome. The structure was octagonal and the dome itself lay in the center with a diameter of sixty-six feet.

By the time he reached the entrance, he was exhausted and huffing wildly. Still, he had made it. He hurried inside.

He then stopped in his tracks. The titular rock made up the majority of the center of the room, and it was surrounded by pillars. But that wasn't what had taken his breath at that moment. The piles of bodies that lay about the room and which had soaked the floor in blood were what stopped him. A dozen Crusaders stood over the bodies. And in the corner, his gaze fell upon the lifeless forms of his wife and children.

The Crusaders turned to face him. Some of them had taken their helmets off, revealing the faces of pure evil. These men smiled at him and gloated in their language. They gestured proudly at the carnage they had inflicted.

All reason left the Muslim then. In fact, everything left him except the unbridled fury which would now be directed against these barbarians. His energy renewed, he charged in, heedless of danger. He arrived at the closest Crusader and nearly took his head off with one swing of his sword.

The other monsters, now realizing they couldn't take him lightly, swiftly closed in on him as one. Their attacks were coordinated, and within moments, they overwhelmed him. They slashed at every inch of his body. As far gone mentally as he was, he felt no pain and continued to struggle. The Crusaders cried out in surprise at his superhuman strength.

Eventually, though, they switched from slashing to stabbing. They ran him through a dozen times with their swords. His blood left his body in great waves.

Finally, he could no longer send commands to his limbs to keep fighting, and he dropped to the ground. The Crusaders exclaimed in their language, but even if he could understand it, he lay there barely conscious.

* * *

His eyes lethargically opened. It took a few moments for his vision to clear enough to see. He lay on his back and a bronzed-skin man was crouched over him. The smell of death was thick.

"Wh.... who... are you?" he managed to say.

"I am a friend," the man replied. He was tanned but not Middle-Eastern and didn't have the barbaric disposition of a Crusader, but that mattered little to Kyrios.

"You speak my language," the Muslim said.

The man replied cryptically, "I have had much time to learn it."

It didn't matter. "Leave me. I have nothing left to live for."

"Yes," the man said sadly. "I don't know who among these was your family, but they have long since passed. But it's not too late for *you*. I can save you.

"Did you not hear me? I have... nothing left," he said.

The man smiled. "Your family has not been avenged. Is that not something to live for?"

He had a point. However... "No... medicine can... save me now. You are wasting your time." He coughed up blood.

"*My* medicine can save you," the man insisted.

"Then, by all means, try it," the Muslim said sardonically.

The man produced a goblet. "Drink this."

He put the goblet to the Muslim's lips. To his surprise, it was blood.

After some... discomfort, he found himself fully healed. He got back to his feet "How did you do that?" he asked, astonished.

"What you just drank was an evolved form of the blood of Christ."

"Surely, you must be joking."

"I am not. Oh! Where are my manners? My name is Claudius. And you, my new friend, have just entered a new world of possibilities."

As long as one of those possibilities was vengeance, he had no complaints.

The defender ventured out into the night to see to that.

* * *

Claudius caught up with him a short distance from the Dome of the Rock in the courtyard. Now he was surrounded by the brutalized bodies of the men who had killed his family. He stared at his blood-soaked hands in amazement. "Before, I stood no chance against them. Now, they had no chance against *me*. What am I?"

Claudius took in the scene with detachment. He had been alive for over a thousand years; he had scene violence countless times. He didn't even notice the smell of death anymore. "I've always called us *sanguinem populum*—Blood People in Latin. Perhaps you can think of a better name. The important thing to note, besides your enhanced strength and speed, is your newfound weakness to sunlight. You must exist as *noctiuagus*—a night walker. Never venture out during the day. In the beginning, things were different, and the sun didn't immediately kill us. But it seems our affliction has been altered over the years in various ways. Perhaps the blood of Christ continues to change even after consumption."

The Muslim shot him a venomous look. "Christ? The god the heathens follow? The one they've done their best to kill us over? Are you telling me it was his blood I drank?" He trembled at the thought. Claudius had mentioned it earlier, but he had paid no heed to his words. Muslims believed Christ was a mere prophet, but the barbarians worshipped him as if he were Allah.

"Technically, it was my blood," Claudius said. "But mine contains the same properties as that of Christ."

He had been made a thrall of the barbaric Christians' god. What sick joke was this? He howled in fury, and Claudius winced at this. The Muslim was about to attack him next when a thought occurred to him. He could use the Christian god's own power against him. He would take this curse and wield it in the name of justice.

"Tell me more," he said to Claudius. Power required knowledge to use effectively, and he was determined to learn all he could about his new condition.

"We should leave the city first," Claudius said. "There are still many more Crusaders here, and even we would have a difficult time against them."

"Let them come. We can deal with them here and now." He knew part of him had died that night. The only thing he felt now was hate and satisfaction at giving in to the hate.

"Don't be a fool. You were only just turned. There are thousands of them ransacking this city."

He replied, "Then there are thousands that must die."

Claudius grabbed his arm. Despite his newfound strength, he found himself powerless to free himself from Claudius' grip. "The fact you cannot escape my power means yours is not yet fully realized. Only your prowess allowed you to overcome these men lying at our feet. I say we are leaving and leave we shall."

The former defender was reluctant to abandon his vengeance, but as he could not overcome Claudius—and as there was nothing left for him here—he went along with his new friend. He did, however, receive a consolation prize as dozens of heathens tried stopping them from leaving. These Claudius allowed him to kill, though Claudius himself withheld from the bloodshed.

As they emerged from the city gates, Claudius asked him, "What is your name?"

"I have no name. The man with a name and family is no more. From this point forward, I will take a new name."

"Very well. What is your new name?" Claudius said.

"I've heard one of the names of the invaders' god is 'Kyrios.' I shall take that name and make it my own. They want a king? I will give them the same kind they gave me."

Claudius said nothing further.

They spent the night in a cave outside the city—the same cave Claudius and Longinus had stayed in after their turning. Claudius told Kyrios about it after they had started a fire. There was no reason to start a fire other than to maintain a semblance of humanity, but they found it comforting regardless.

"And where were you all the years since then?" Kyrios asked.

Claudius shrugged. "I have spent the bulk of my life traveling the world and seeing all there is to see. I consider myself a student of humanity. The Crusades brought me back to Jerusalem. I was curious to see the war between Christians and Muslims. What a truly violent thing religion is."

"*Their* religion is violent. They invaded *us.*" There was no simpler truth in this world. Claudius had to see that.

"Ah," Claudius said, "but did not Abu Ubaidah invade first in 636? Do not delude yourself into thinking Islam is any more peaceful than Christianity. All of the monotheistic religions are perverse."

"*We* were peaceful," Kyrios insisted. "My family and I, we never hurt anyone. Nor did any of our friends. It was the Christians who brought death and destruction to our land."

"I am sorry for your loss. My family died of old age so I cannot relate to what you've been through."

Kyrios still trembled. The murder of his family remained fresh in his mind. He gripped his head with both hands and began wailing.

Claudius continued. "At least you saw that justice was done. The men who killed your loved ones are no more."

He concluded Claudius was right about religion being a violent thing. But only one religion had taken everything from him tonight. Justice was far from done. Christianity wasn't any one person; it was an idea that caused madness. It was a disease.

And diseases needed to be cured.

* * *

January 23, 1523 A.D.

Claudius and Kyrios strode along Upper Thames Street a little bit north of the Thames river in London. Ostensibly, they had come here so Kyrios could learn about Christians and possibly come to accept them. That was what Claudius believed, anyway; in actuality, Kyrios had wanted to come here to learn about his *enemies*. He wanted to know their infrastructure, economics, belief systems, etc.

After all these centuries, Claudius was still indifferent to the Christian plague and tried to avoid violence whenever possible. He was soft, and Kyrios knew one day he might have to leave his friend's company to pursue his true goals.

The shahid—as Kyrios now called them—had established a thriving civilization in the shadows of Jerusalem. Claudius and Kyrios had returned when Muslims regained control of the city. When the day-dwellers went to sleep, the Holy Land's other society arose.

But at that moment, they were 3,610 kilometers away in another world. The snow from one of England's bitter winters was packed beneath their feet on the cobblestone streets and crunched as they walked. It showed no sign of letting up anytime soon.

They stopped in front of a church that consisted of a square building and a large tower in front. The sign said "St. Mary's Somerset."

"There is a light on inside," Claudius said. "We could go in and say hello."

Kyrios was more interested in saying goodbye to whoever was in there. However, his attention was grabbed by the faint sound of breathing. Peering around, he saw no one other than Claudius. It was then he noticed a minuscule heat signature on the steps of the church. "Someone is sitting there," he marveled and pointed. Claudius followed his finger to a figure sitting curled up on the steps. This person was almost completely covered by snow.

"Hello?" Claudius said. There was no response.

Kyrios brushed the snow off and uncovered the outline of a woman. She stared at him with lifeless eyes. "She obviously froze to death."

"But why?" Claudius said. "Couldn't she have gone into the church for shelter?"

Kyrios was about to venture a guess when the presumed corpse grabbed his arm. Even more amazing, she spoke. "Leave me." Her voice was ragged and her mouth chattered from the cold.

It had been a long time since anyone had intrigued Kyrios like this. He wanted to know more, but this wasn't the proper place for introductions.

He scooped her up in his arms and marched into the church where it was, not warm exactly, but considerably less cold. He laid her down on a pew.

"What are you doing?" an angry priest came over and asked. He was fat and balding.

"This woman needs medical attention. Call a doctor," Kyrios said.

The priest pointed an accusing finger at her. "Not for *this* woman. She is not allowed in any church in England."

"Why not?" Claudius said.

"She is in league with the Devil," he spat.

In league with the enemy of God? Kyrios was enjoying her company more and more as the minutes went on.

"What do you mean?" Claudius said.

"They say she practices sorcery. If we could prove it, we would put her to death."

"Death?" Kyrios said. "For not sharing your values? How completely... Christian."

The priest folded his arms. "It seems clear to me that you two aren't from England. As you are outsiders trying to save a witch, I must ask you to leave at once."

Kyrios moved to snap his neck, but Claudius grabbed his arm. "Now is not the time." The priest fell back, terror shining in his eyes.

Seething, Kyrios fought a titanic battle to control himself. He looked down at the woman who would probably die any moment. There wasn't time to send for a doctor even if the priest had been willing. That only left one option.

Kyrios had long nails. He clenched his hand into a tight fist until he drew blood. He then opened the woman's mouth with his other hand and sprinkled the blood into it.

"What are you doing?" Claudius said. He had a rule against turning people against their will, but Kyrios didn't care.

"What does it look like? I am saving her."

"That's not for you to decide!"

Caught somewhere between consciousness and a dream state, she must have thought she was being fed water. She gulped down the blood.

"You fool!" Claudius said. "She had already given us her decision. You have now condemned her to be a slave to the night."

Perhaps, but now she would be able to tell Kyrios her story. At the moment, that was all he cared about. His desire to know her was something beyond his understanding.

A soft glow emanated and the ice melted off her. She thrashed about, her eyes still closed. Within moments, her skin returned to normal and the thrashing subsided. The priest recoiled in horror. "Demons!" He ran over and grabbed an oak cross off the walls which he waved at them as if his misguided beliefs alone would be enough to hurt them. Kyrios took it from him and crushed it in his hand. He flung the pieces to the floor and crushed them further under his foot. Still not satisfied, he proceeded to stomp them into dust.

"What is the meaning of this?" the woman said behind him.

Kyrios turned around to find her sitting up on the pew, chunks of snow falling off her simple clothing. Her face was still wet. "Just a difference of opinion." Just a moment before, it was about to be a fatal one.

She arched an eyebrow and looked around hopelessly. "Who are you? Why did you save me? *How* did you save me?"

"That requires a great deal of explanation," Claudius said. The doors of the church burst open and the priest shot out into the night, probably to look for a constable. Or a great many people to form a mob with. "We should probably continue this conversation elsewhere."

But before they could leave, Kyrios asked her, "What is your name?"

She was busy looking over her now-frostbite-free limbs. "What? Oh? I'm Ursula. Ursula Southeil."

Kyrios extended his hand. "Come with us, Ursula. We will show you a world free of religious oppression. A world without men like that priest."

Her eyes darted back and forth between him and Claudius. Finally, she took Kyrios' hand and he brought her to her feet. "I have never seen such a world. You had better not be lying."

"When it comes to freeing the oppressed," he said, "I never lie." He then turned to Claudius. "I think we have learned enough here. It's time we went home."

"And where is home?" Ursula said.

"Jerusalem," Claudius said. "The journey will take a fair bit of time."

She smiled. "As long as it gets me out of England, I'll go wherever you want. I trust you have passage on a ship?"

Inwardly, Kyrios smiled. Indeed, they did, and he felt shahid and ocean travel would have an interesting dynamic as time went on.

10

Ursula stared at the lifeless husk that had been dumped in front of her in their cabin, revulsion showing plainly on her face. Kyrios didn't care; shahid needed to feed like anyone else. They had survived on rats for most of the voyage, but bad weather had delayed their return to Jerusalem. Now, with the rodents gone, they had no choice but to subsist on humans. They had been traveling aboard the ship in coffins. Kyrios and Claudius had decided upon this method of shipping because coffins were designed to hold people and blocked out the sun.

"Eat," Kyrios said.

She was visibly mortified by the corpse of the deckhand. His eyes were still bulging out of his head, a look of terror reaching out from beyond the grave.

"I can't," she said, trembling.

"You have no choice," Kyrios said as he stood over them. "With our humane source of sustenance gone, this is what's left to us."

She answered with, "You killed him."

"I did."

"Then, how are you any different from the Christians that took your family from you?"

He had thought this over many times and had prepared a careful rationale in case anyone challenged him on it. "They kill to satisfy a fairy tale. They kill because their holy book, the Bible, tells them to. *We* kill merely to survive. We are no different than the hunters who must feed their tribe. We leave religion out of it whenever possible."

She continued to stare into the lifeless eyes of the deckhand. Their questioning gaze haunted her.

They seemed to say, *What did I do to deserve this?* She was still trembling, but not from fear. She trembled from hunger.

Claudius, who had been sitting silently on the bunk, "I'm sorry, Ursula, but you must. And while it is true Kyrios is responsible for your current situation, his crime is turning you without your permission. Blame him for that."

"I'll thank you to be quiet," Kyrios said while glaring at him.

Finally, Ursula said, "Where should I...?" while studying the corpse.

"Avoid the neck, as I have already fed from there. If a shahid sticks their fangs into the same holes of another shahid, it transmits a disease that can kill even us. *Repetita residuam languorem,* our doctors call it. I call it the Rot. As long as you avoid the holes I made, you'll be fine."

✱ ✱ ✱

Later that night, Kyrios found Ursula standing against the ship's railing staring out at the sea. The water crashed futilely against the hull, releasing a light mist that washed over the two of them. A full moon hung overhead, the merciful antithesis to the orb that damned them during the day. The salty fragrance of sea water pleased his sense of smell. Out here, no enemies could be found as they had disposed of the entire crew. Unfortunately, this meant they had to man the vessel themselves, requiring them to drop anchor during the day.

"We should reach Jerusalem tomorrow," he said as he took up position beside her.

"I can't wait to get off this ship," she replied while continuing to stare into the sea.

"If you don't mind my asking, why were you persecuted in your homeland?"

"I didn't practice the approved medicine," she said. "I looked beyond the close-minded system and sought to treat others with an approach that was, shall we say, not quite holy."

To his surprise, he smiled. "You were a healer, then?"

She nodded. "A very successful one, I might add. Unfortunately, that only added to the suspicion the more devout citizens around me already held. Nevertheless, I firmly believe in saving people. That's why it was so hard to feed on the crew of this vessel. I want to preserve life, not take it."

"I apologize. I wish the circumstances had been otherwise. It seems no matter where we go in this world, we encounter contradictions. I wanted to save my family, but I had to kill to even attempt to do so."

She turned to look at him. "Your family. What were they like?"

He explained, "My wife was strong and full of fire. I am certain she made the invaders pay for every ounce of blood they took from her and our children. You remind me of her.

"We had two sons. They both wanted to follow me and become city guards when they came of age."

"I deeply apologize for your loss. I suppose it was my people—the Europeans—that did it, though I don't consider myself one of them."

He wanted to touch her. He was taken aback by his strong feelings for her. He had only known her a short time, but he longed to spend every waking hour with her. But why? He hadn't given any thought to starting a new family, and he certainly hadn't gotten close to any woman in all the years since his turning. But she had the same fire his wife had possessed, and that drew him in relentlessly. "Be at ease. I don't hold you responsible for something that was done centuries ago. You are as far above those monsters as they were to insects."

"That is high praise indeed. I hope I'll continue to live up to your words."

"I believe you shall."

They stopped talking as he fantasized about a life with her. Perhaps, just perhaps, he would find happiness again.

* * *

Beneath Jerusalem, there was a complex tunnel system under the Western Wall. Labyrinthine corridors stretched from one side of the city to the other. This was where the vampiric side of humanity governed.

Torches lined the ancient rock walls, giving the tunnels a grim illumination. Large shadows were cast by everyone going to and fro. Some areas were large enough to hold dozens of people, while others were the width of only a single person, requiring inhabitants to walk single file.

Kyrios and Claudius led Ursula through the corridors to a modest square meeting hall. The decorations here were sparse, only what the shahid needed to function. Presently, ten people were lounging around, a few of them smoking from hookahs. They jumped to attention when their leader entered the room. "Everyone, we have a new member joining us today. Her name is Ursula Southeil. Ursula, these are Amelie, Mikhail, Cortez, Ahmad, Basheer, Faysal, Imad, Naeem, and Irfan."

"Pleased to meet you," Amelie said, extending her hand which Ursula accepted.

"Hello," Mikhail said half-heartedly.

The rest of the shahid merely stared at her. They were, of course, leery of outsiders, while Amelia could sympathize because *she* had once been an outsider. Mikhail was simply prickly.

"Your attire is interesting," Ursula said. "How did you decide on red robes?"

Kyrios explained, "The red symbolizes the blood that has been shed by those oppressed by religious tyranny. The cloaks hide our identities when we strike back at the oppressors."

Amelie went over to the corner, opened a wicker basket, and retrieved an identical robe before returning to Ursula. "You have been oppressed as well, or else Kyrios would not have invited you to join us. Here."

"Thank you." She took the robe and smiled.

Without warning, though, Ursula cried out in pain and dropped to her knees, one hand gripping her forehead.

"What is it?" Claudius said, concerned.

"I-I don't know," she said.

They helped her up, and she stared. "Are you all right?" Kyrios said.

"I... believe so." She continued to stare, and that concerned him.

She was staring at *him* with a wild look in her eyes. *Why does she view me with fear?* he wondered.

She finally looked away. "I think I need to lie down," she said.

"Yes, of course. Amelie, show her to her floor mat," Kyrios said.

* * *

Months passed, and Ursula settled in underneath Jerusalem. While she was friendly with most of the shahid, she remained distant from Kyrios. He didn't know why, and that troubled him. What was it about him that scared her so? Yes, he harbored a hatred of Christians, but so did most of the people in the under-city.

One day, Claudius came to the manzil's room in the corridors. Claudius himself wasn't part of the manzil as he had his hands full helping run the shahid shadow government in the tunnels, but he still counted Kyrios as a close friend.

Kyrios had lately been writing down his thoughts and experiences. He had a small table in the room he shared with the rest of the manzil, and on this night he was engaged in that. All of the other members were out enjoying the city's nightlife. He cared little for merriment. But more than that, being out in Jerusalem's streets reminded him of his murdered family and the happiness they used to share. Sometimes, he wondered if they shouldn't move their capital to somewhere—anywhere—else. Even barbaric London would have been a less depressing locale, and there would be more deserving victims to feed on.

He looked up when Claudius entered the room. His friend wore a serious expression. "There's something I need to tell you, Kyrios."

"What is it?"

"Ursula has left Jerusalem and returned to England."

"What?" Kyrios leapt to his feet. "Why?"

Claudius frowned. "I'm not certain. She simply said this place troubled her."

You mean I troubled her. "Did she elaborate in any way?"

"Only to say she didn't belong here and her destiny lay elsewhere."

Kyrios delivered a savage kick to the wooden table, shattering it and sending the various pieces crashing into the stone wall. "Why couldn't she accept me? I did everything I could to appeal to her!"

But Claudius said, "You are taking this too personally. It is not a reflection on you. Not everyone takes to Jerusalem. We've had people leave before."

Too personally? How should I take it, then? I know in my heart it was because of me. I came on too strong, or perhaps it was some quirk of mine that drove her away. "I wanted to moonlight bond with her."

"Oh," Claudius said, surprised. "I had assumed that, after what happened to your previous mate, you would not want to do so again. You never expressed any interest in starting a new family."

Kyrios replied, "I was afraid of looking like a fool if rejected. And she had been avoiding me, anyway. I saw no reason to bring it up."

Claudius put a comforting hand on Kyrios' shoulder. "I am sorry, my friend. But now that you are open to moonlight bonding, other opportunities will come."

Kyrios stared at the splintered remains of the table lying in a heap against the wall. "That is of little comfort at the moment."

11

Kyle awoke with a start. *What was that? I was dreaming about Kyrios and Christ. Did all that happen?* Ursula had said Kyle would find out about Kyrios on his own. Was this what she had been referring to?

It was night now. The only illumination came from the legion of lights of the city. New York was such a far cry from Perry, Oklahoma, a sleepy town of fewer than ten thousand people. It was a beast not unlike its more demonic inhabitants. Well, at least they had Lake Carl Blackwell near Perry.

There was a knock at the door. Kyle tensed up. "Who is it?"

"Me," came Chloe's voice. "Forgot keys."

Relieved, he turned on the lamp next to the couch and headed over to let her in. Sure enough, it was Chloe on the other side. "Appreciate it."

"You're welcome."

She walked past him and he moved to close the door. He was then grabbed from behind, decidedly masculine hands wrapping around his neck. "What are you doing?" he yelled.

A large man appeared and stood in the doorway. "Well done, 'Chloe,'" he said in a Russian accent while grinning up a storm. He wore a chain mesh shirt and black latex pants. His head was shaved nearly bald. He had a tattoo of the stereotypical devil on his neck.

"Let's just get this over with," the person holding Kyle said in an Irish accent. Chloe hadn't betrayed him, then. Or maybe she had and her true form was a man.

The Russian removed an ice pick from his pants and held it aloft. "We have plenty of time. We kill Jesus brat and then we dispose of albino bitch."

"I thought Kyrios wanted me alive to be his soldier or something," Kyle said. He tried to sound cool but he was scared to death.

"Kyrios made mistake," the Russian said. "We are here to put manzil back on track, as you Americans say."

"I'm sorry about this," the Irishman said. "But if we don't, we'll be sanctioned. That's a polite way of saying we'll be flayed alive for twenty-four hours straight. It's not enough to kill our kind, but it'll make you wish it was."

That sucked, but Kyle had no intention of being murdered for it. Ironically, he had to help Kyrios by taking care of his more traitorous minions.

He raised his legs and shoved them into the Russian as hard as he could. This resulted in everyone flying backward. Kyle and the Irishman fell back onto a coffee table which didn't stand a chance. It was annihilated with a thunderous crash. The Irishman groaned.

Kyle wasted no time getting to his feet. The shattered glass crunched under him. He grabbed a shard and winced as it sliced his hand. He didn't have time for pain, though. He turned around and slammed the shard into the Irishman's chest. His enemy's eyes went wide and a sharp breath escaped him. He wasn't sure exactly where the heart was, so he just had to guess and hoped this guy stayed down long enough for him to deal with the Russian.

With the Irishman incapacitated, Kyle turned around to face the Russian who was getting back on his feet just outside the doorway. Kyle rushed him.

He didn't get far, however. Without warning, he was struck down by an intense feeling of vertigo. He lost all his equilibrium and fell flat on his face.

"Never attack opponent when you don't know Satanic Gift," the Russian said. He strode over and picked up the ice pick which lay next to Kyle's head. He then grabbed Kyle by the hair and lifted him to his feet. Once back on his feet, Kyle struggled to stay that way. But was all he could do; he couldn't mount any attacks against his enemy. The Russian, meanwhile, was all too happy to help by holding onto Kyle's hair.

The Russian flipped the pick around so he could more easily stab Kyle with it. He put the sharp end to Kyle's chest. "You will die slowly. I will insert ice pick into your heart millimeter by millimeter."

He put the tip of the pick to Kyle's chest. There was little pain at first, but then he went deeper. Kyle cried out as the Russian began twisting. Any moment now, the pick would reach his heart. He noted with gallows humor the wooden stake was a little outdated, he supposed.

A bright blue light appeared behind the Russian and he screamed before falling to his feet revealing Chloe. She rushed in and took hold of the pick, ripping it out of Kyle's chest. Kyle fell into her arms, still dazed from the Russian's Satanic Gift.

She lowered him to his knees. "All... right?"

"I-I think so."

"Fucking bitch!" the Russian yelled. In response, an electric knife materialized in her hand and she flicked it at his head. Kyle looked away, not wanting to see the results, but he heard both a bang and a splatter sound.

Chloe went over to check on the Irishman. "Good... aim."

He had found the heart after all. He was officially a killer now. There wasn't time for him to reflect on that, because she hurried back and said, "Must... leave."

$$* * *$$

They once again found themselves in an alley. Sirens blared in the distance. That was now a common occurrence in New York City. Or maybe it always was. "Thanks for saving me."

They sat next to one another against the wall of a building. "Couldn't... let die. Would have... done same."

"I mean, I would have tried. I don't have my Satanic Gift yet."

"Thought that... counts."

"I guess you're right." He was silent for a moment. "I killed that guy. Does it ever get easier?"

"No. You... will... ungh... hurt."

He sighed. "And we still have a bunch more of them to kill."

"Must... be... ungh... done."

He looked at her. "I don't know if I can do this. It's too much."

She smiled at him. "Can do. You... strong."

That made him feel better. "Well, thanks. But now we're back where we started. We don't have anywhere to go."

"Safe houses... not safe."

"They're definitely not. And I don't know many people here. The only other person is..."

"Yes?"

"Hmmm. How did you track me to the church?"

"Saw you... leaving bar."

"That's what I thought. Okay, so that bar has the only other person I know here. It's a long shot, but we could try there."

"Will... work?"

He got up. "I have a feeling God will provide," he said optimistically.

As if to challenge that notion, both ends of the alley were blocked by police cars, their lights flashing a threatening sonata of red and blue. Two cops got out of each car for a total of four. They pointed their guns at Kyle and Chloe. "Get on the ground, hands on your head!" God seemed to be taking his time.

The two vampires put their hands up. "Don't shoot!" Kyle said. "We'll cooperate!"

"On the ground!"

"Can't... get... ungh... arrested."

Kyle eased down to his knees. She followed. "I know, but what can we do?"

The four cops strode over to them, their weapons at the ready. "We're going to detain you for questioning," one said.

Two of the others produced zip-tie handcuffs and secured Kyle and Chloe with them. They then made them lie on their stomachs.

The first guy continued. "There were murders here just now. What do you know about them?"

"Hey, we're just two homeless people looking for shelter. We only just got here," Kyle said. He was becoming more comfortable with lying, a fact that scared him slightly. Like transforming not into a monster per se, but into a crappier version of yourself.

"That's... true."

"I think this one might be on drugs," one of the other cops said of Chloe.

"Am... not!"

"Let's take them in," the interrogator said.

The cops dragged them to their feet. All four officers gathered together to keep their persons of interest from causing trouble.

Big mistake.

Chloe ripped her cuffs apart like a paper bag and performed a palm strike on one of the cops holding her. Kyle did the same, and within moments, all of the boys in blue were incapacitated. "Let's not kill them. They were only doing their job," Kyle said.

Chloe reminded him, "Hate... killing."

"Right. Let's get out of here before more show up."

Before leaving, he spared a glance at the fallen police officers in the alley. Kyle had gone easy on them, but he still felt things break. This wasn't like the movies. You couldn't just karate-chop someone in the back of the neck to knock them out. You had to use real, dangerous force. There would undoubtedly be injuries because of this incident. But at least there wouldn't be any more violence tonight.

Kyle noticed too late the *thump-thump-thump* of a helicopter in the area. His mind had been elsewhere. But it swooped over the building shining its spotlight down below. When said spotlight hit the alley and the operator noticed the fallen officers, the chopper focused on that spot. A booming voice shouted, "This is the police! Get on the ground with your hands behind your head!"

Kyle used one arm to shield his face. With the other, he motioned to Chloe to run. They began their sprint out of there and Kyle pulled his shirt over his head to hide his identity.

They emerged from the alley onto a busy intersection. Cars and other assorted modes of transportation were coming and going from all directions. Sedans; busses; trucks; bicycles; vans; all were fully represented here. People of all races and genders moved back and forth on the crosswalks. Most of them stopped to look up and marvel at the helicopter which was now shining a light down on them.

Kyle and Chloe dashed around cars and leapt over the ones they couldn't avoid. "Thief... in... Night!" she said.

He would totally have done that, but it required time to concentrate he didn't have. The 'copter was keeping pace with them and didn't look like it would be letting up any time soon.

They continued running across city streets and through busy areas. More cop cars appeared ahead of them, their sirens blaring a threatening symphony.

"Climb... up!" Chloe said, pointing to a ten-story brick bank. They ran over and struck their hands into the wall to make handholds. The police cars arrived within moments but the officers were left slack-jawed at the sight above them.

The vampiric pair soon reached the roof. "What now? We're trapped," Kyle said.

In response, Chloe produced a single lightning knife. "Whoa, whoa, whoa," Kyle said, thinking she was going to fight their way out of this.

"Trust... me."

She focused on the knife. It became smaller and less vibrant until it shone a dull blue. She then flicked it at the helicopter. It hit the searchlight, shattering it and causing it to go out. The rest of the chopper seemed unaffected but it pulled out anyway presumably to avoid any more projectiles. "Now... time."

Thankful to her, he closed his eyes and concentrated. They activated Thief in the Night and promptly made their escape.

* * *

Angelica looked over the body of Martha Shipton inside St. Martin's Medical Center, a hospital in New York funded by the Vatican. They were in a cold, sterile, metallic room. Angelica wore a green lab coat and matching scrubs. A recorder on the wall was running. The body of Shipton lay on a rubber block.

As a Redeemer, Angelica had been given extensive medical training to identify vampires. She was well into the procedure now, having removed Shipton's rib cage.

She spoke into a recorder. She had already noted the immediate details about Shipton's body, including her fangs. "As expected, subject has an enlarged heart consistent with *Cristo Malattia del Sangue.* Also consistent with the disease is the enhanced durability of the body. If not for my own enhanced strength, I would have had great difficulty carrying out this procedure.

"Subject's cause of death is the destruction of the heart via high voltage. She was not killed by a Redeemer, so I can only conclude the killer was another vampire. My current hypothesis is the decedent angered the vampire group that seems to have kidnapped Kyle Falconer by rescuing him. The kidnappers sent one of their own to get revenge. The one chosen for the job has a Satanic Gift that utilizes some form of electricity. This will be crucial information going forward.

"There is a tattoo of an eye crying blood on her neck. This is the emblem of our *other* enemy, the

Siren Sisterhood. I never thought we'd find someone who was both. If they're involved with this, the situation could be direr than we thought. Worst case scenario: the vampires and the Sisterhood working together. I need to inform the Vatican as soon as I finish here."

Her cell phone rang, cutting off her train of thought. She answered it.

"This is Rourke. Thought you'd be interested to know there were a few more killings tonight."

"There are always killings in this city, Detective," she said testily. "How does this relate to my investigation?"

"The victims both have fangs."

"You should have led with that, Detective. What happened?"

He explained, "There was a commotion in an apartment not too far from your position. First responders found two bodies. One had a shard of glass through the heart, and the other had wounds consistent with Martha Shipton's."

"Interesting," she said. "Any witnesses?"

"Not to the actual killings, no. But four of my fellow cops got their asses handed to them by two people matching the description of Kyle Falconer and the albino girl. They then led one of our choppers on a merry chase before making their escape."

"I'm sorry for the casualties you suffered. Rest assured; they will be avenged."

But he said, "That's the thing, though. Falconer and the albino didn't kill *any* cops tonight. In fact, they seemed to go out of their way to avoid it."

That didn't make sense. Both of them were hell spawn; why wouldn't they enjoy the taking of

122

innocent lives? "Give me the location and I will head over there at once."

* * *

Kyle peered out from behind a bus stop stand. "How... is?" Chloe asked him.

"Well, I don't see any of our enemies, but that doesn't mean they're not around." In fact, the area in front of Mel's was the same as it had been on previous visits. The sounds of the city reverberated through the area. Cars honked; people guffawed loudly at stupid things; idiots driving by blasted heavy bass from their tricked-out sound systems; many conversations were going on between people.

"I guess we have no choice but to go over there."

The two of them crossed the street, weaving between cars and constantly looking left and right, left and right, left and right for any signs of their enemies. Everything looked normal, though.

When they made it to Mel's, Kyle caught sight of a sign in the window. It was a picture of the Redeemer taken from the overhead security camera. Above it read, **"NOT ALLOWED ON PREMISES."** Kyle breathed a sigh of relief at the knowledge she was banned. Of course, that didn't mean Kyle *wasn't*.

"That's the Redeemer," Kyle said, pointing at the sign.

"Never seen... Redeemer. Only... heard."

They went inside and made their way over to the bar where Jazmine was tending. "Hi," Kyle said nervously.

Jazmine raised an eyebrow at the sight of him. "Well, looks who's back. I'm stuck with the repair bill for that door your crazy friend broke."

"She's *not* my friend. Far from it."

"Well, she certainly seemed to know you."

"It's complicated," Kyle said.

But Jazmine said, "You know when things aren't complicated? After you explain them."

"Wouldn't... believe," Chloe said.

Jazmine seemed to notice her for the first time at that moment. She looked at her before addressing Kyle. "I think I owe you an apology, Sour Cream."

"Chloe's right," Kyle said. "I don't think you'd believe us."

Jazmine looked back and forth between Kyle and Chloe. "And who's this girl?"

Kyle didn't even know how to answer that. Aside from being a vampire which Jazmine wouldn't believe, what was she to him?

Chloe answered for him. "Friend." Did she honestly consider him a friend, or was she making it up to fool Jazmine?

"I thought you only knew two other people in New York. One of them's mysterious, and the other's a homicidal psychopath. Which are you, girl?"

"Homicidal... psychopath," she said matter-of-factly. Kyle's face must have been turning red to see her find out what he initially thought of her.

"It's not like that," he said. "I mean, I thought it was, but then I found out she's actually nice."

Jazmine stared at them for a moment. "I think we'd better discuss this in my office." They went to the back. "Now, then. Who was that crazy lady from the other night?"

"Like I said, you wouldn't believe us."

"Oh, yeah? Here's what I believe. I believe that woman was either a vampire or a Redeemer. Now, which is it?"

Kyle was dumbfounded. "Y-You know about vampires?"

She put her hands on her hips. "Bitch, please. Everyone in this room is a vampire."

Kyle gaped at her. "You mean...?"

"Why do you think this place is only open at night? And you two are pale as hell. Especially her."

"Rude."

"Well, I'm sorry, but I have to cut through the bullshit here."

"But you don't have fangs," Kyle said.

Jazmine pulled at her teeth and removed some sort of plastic mold in the shape of ordinary teeth around her fangs. "You just put these in, and no one can tell the difference."

Kyle managed to recover his composure. "I had no idea."

Jazmine got smug all of a sudden. "Then the false teeth did their job. Now, tell me what's going on."

Kyle responded, "Okay, a vampiric madman is plotting to start a holy war by killing the Grand Imam when he comes to town. Chloe here used to work for him but has since joined me to stop him. Because of his Satanic Gift, neither of us can attack him directly, and he has henchmen, so we need more manpower to prevent an apocalypse."

Jazmine whistled. "That's a hell of a story, Sour Cream."

"Yeah, but it's true. We have to stop Kyrios from inciting a holy war, but we can't do it alone. We need help."

"Well, I'd say you just found it."

"What? Just like that?"

"Not... joking?"

"Not one bit. You see, a year ago, a British vampire came in and sat down at the bar. She told me this exact situation would happen around this time. She told me other things, too. And everything she said came true."

"Must have been Ursula," Kyle said. "Her Gift is the ability to see the future."

Jazmine raised an index finger. "That would explain it.

"We have a loft above the bar. You can use it as your base. I'll take you up there after I close."

Kyle bowed profusely. "Thank you so much! I wasn't sure if God would provide for us."

"Hmph. Well, I'll leave my views on God out of this."

"Appreciate," Chloe said.

They waited around until closing time and then helped Jazmine clean up. Kyle stuck close to Chloe, although he wasn't sure why. He felt he had to protect her. It was the same thing he had felt for Ursula, and he couldn't explain it. Chloe didn't seem to mind, though. Jazmine served them blood cocktails. Kyle didn't ask where the blood came from. He was developing a taste for it, a fortunate situation for a vampire.

When they were done, Jazmine took them upstairs. "Nice!" Kyle said upon seeing it. The loft was two floors. On the first floor in front of them was a living room area with the biggest TV Kyle had ever seen in front of the largest couch he had ever seen. To their right was a kitchen area with every appliance one would ever need. To their left was a staircase leading up to the next floor.

"Welcome home!" A black woman with a buzz cut, wearing an orange cocktail dress, came over to greet Jazmine. Whereas Jazmine was slim, this person was what they called a BBW—big, beautiful woman.

They kissed. "How was your session?" Jazmine said.

The stranger was smiling. "Knocked 'em out, as always." She then noticed the interlopers for the first time. "You've never brought home white people before."

"Oh, sorry! Mel, this is Kyle and Chloe. Kyle and Chloe, this is Mel."

"Nice to meet you," Kyle said. Chloe just nodded.

"Umm, nice to meet you two," Mel said, clearly caught off guard.

"I know it's short notice, but I told them they could stay with us for a bit. I hope that's okay?"

"Well... I mean... sure. Any friend of Jazmine's is a friend of mine, I guess."

"Thank you!" Kyle said.

"No... bother?"

"No, it's fine," Mel said. "How long were you planning on staying...?"

Kyle shrugged. "We have no idea. We're both sort of homeless right now."

"Riiiiiight." She tried to hide it, but they were an imposition.

Jazmine put her palms together. "It'll be fine. You'll see. Oh, and I told them we would help them stop a holy war."

"Wait, what?" They explained it to her. "Oh. I see. And you thought you'd volunteer us for something that could get us killed. Sure, why not!"

"Please don't be like that," Jazmine said.

"And how, exactly, should I be? These white people come in and tell you there's going to be a holy war, and you believe them? Based on what?"

"That British woman said this would happen, remember?"

"I don't care. We are not having this conversation right now." Mel stormed off.

Kyle grimaced. "That could have gone better."

"We're asking a lot of her all of a sudden. She'll calm down. Just give her time. Right now, there's a guest bedroom upstairs. Follow me."

She led them to the top of the staircase where the promised room awaited. The main color of it was brown. Brown carpet, brown walls, and brown sheets on the queen-sized bed. There were also photos of jazz musicians framed on the walls.

"I'm going to go talk with Mel. You two make yourselves at home." She left Kyle alone with Chloe.

"This isn't too bad," he said. "I just hope Mel doesn't kick us out."

"Nothing... Can... ungh... do. Oh... forgot." She reached into her pocket and pulled out a sheet of paper. She handed it to him.

Hello, Kyle. There's something I need you to do for me. Please follow these directions.

1.) Sit on the floor

2.) Extend your hands palm-first

3.) Close your eyes and visualize a private world for just the two of us

This seemed like a strange request, but what the hell. He sat down. Chloe did the same a few feet in front of him. He stuck out his hands. She matched his movements and touched her palms to his. A rush of excitement surged through him even though he barely knew her.

He closed his eyes and pictured a self-contained space with the two of them that was the only thing in the universe.

"You can open your eyes now."

Surprised to hear her speaking normally, he snapped back to reality. Except "reality" might have been subjective. They were now standing in a different room. This one looked much older, white with no modern items, and posters of 1950s music idols on the wall. "Where are we?"

She was smiling. "My room when I was a kid, except not really. Welcome... to *Alsakina.*" She whirled around, spreading her arms and gesturing to the room.

"Yeah, that doesn't entirely answer the question. What is this place? And why can you speak normally here?"

She explained, "This is a special place for those who have moonlight-bonded."

"Moonlight what?"

"Moonlight bonding. Vampire bonding. You see, our kind doesn't just thirst for blood. We also thirst for intimacy. We crave companionship. Surely, you've noticed the strong feelings you have for me. Don't think I couldn't tell. Well, this space exists only for us in our own minds. Using this, we can bond more deeply than we'd be able to in the real world. Even more deeply than humans can.

Kyle felt he had to point out the obvious. "But you barely know me. Surely, there's someone closer to you."

The smile abruptly faded. She shook her head sadly. "I've been starved for so long, Kyle. No one in the manzil would bond with me. I hated them anyway. I won't force you, but please consider it."

He would be lying if he said he wasn't interested. However, this was all so new to him. "So, you want me because there's no one else?"

She shook her head again, only this time the smile returned. "No, Kyle. You have such strength inside you. You didn't kill me even when your life was threatened. That takes moral strength."

"But I *tried* to."

"Perhaps, but you had the chance to try again shortly thereafter, and you didn't. You basically shrugged off your hatred of me. I thought, if you could let go of violence, I could, too."

"I think you just reached your breaking point, the point where you couldn't deal with it anymore," Kyle offered.

"Maybe, but my point about your inner strength is still valid. You're kind, Kyle. You fought to avenge a woman you had only known for a few days. Not many people would have done that."

"That's true. Okay, then, how does this, like, you know, work?"

"We'll go slow. I think this is enough for our first time. I mostly wanted to introduce you to Alsakina. Now, close your eyes and imagine yourself back in the real world."

He did so. When he reopened them, they were once again sitting on the floor in Jazmine and Mel's guest room. "Wow, that was something."

She was still smiling. "Good?"

"Yeah. I think it was."

"Good." Her eyes closed for a moment before re-opening.

Kyle laughed. "Yeah, me too. Almost being killed tonight took a lot out of me."

"Sleep."

"You can take the bed." Kyle grabbed a pillow and lay on the floor. "Oh, this is a hard floor."

Chloe pulled back the sheets and got in. She patted the side of the bed closest to him. "Come... up."

That made him nervous. "Are you sure?"

"Don't... on... floor."

"Well, okay." He got up and stood staring at the bed. Unmarried men and women weren't supposed to sleep in the same bed, but he would be lying if he said he wasn't tempted.

She nodded. "Come. Don't... worry. Nothing... funny."

Having been assured, he said, "All right." He got in next to her but still left some space between them. It felt good. It felt wrong. He barely knew her, but as she said, vampires had stronger feelings than humans. It helped that he understood his own feelings much better now. "Alsakina, huh? That's pretty wild."

"See more... soon. Hope... so."

"Yeah. But I think for now we should focus on stopping Kyrios."

"Understand."

12

December 7.

Kyle opened his eyes.

"Finally awake, are we?"

Mel stood over him. Chloe was gone. "How long was I asleep?"

Now she was wearing a red cocktail dress instead of an orange one. "You slept all damn day."

He sat up. "I want to apologize for being such an imposition."

"Enough," she said. "We need to talk. I'm heading to work soon, but we have time now. I tried talking with that albino girl, but I didn't get far. You, at least, can keep up with a conversation."

They went down to the bar where Jazmine was tending and sat down. "Two bloody margaritas, Jaz."

"Anything for you, Cocoa."

Jazmine served them red drinks. "Bloody" was very much an apt description of them. "This is a special drink just for our undead customers."

Mel got the conversation started. "Here's the deal, kid. You come in off the street and ask us to help save the world. But we don't even know you. And it's a religious war you want to stop. Now, Jaz and I aren't religious. At all. Churchgoers have made it quite clear we aren't their kind of people. You know how many times we've turned on the TV and seen news coverage of so-called Christians holding signs that say 'God Hates Fags'? That's not exactly endearing to us."

Lately, Kyle had been forced to face the dark side of his religion. "I know Christianity has a lot of problems. We don't always act the way we should. But it's not just Christians that are in danger here. Kyrios is trying to drag Muslims into his war as well."

She snickered. "Muslims? The guys who have the prayer 'Thank Allah I wasn't born a woman'?"

"Well..."

"You'll have to do better than that, Sour Cream, if you want to convince Cocoa," Jazmine said.

"All right, look," Kyle said. "This war won't stop at just those two religions. Fanatics on both sides will target anyone they think is the enemy faith. I've studied history. In times of war, people get paranoid. They strike at anyone who could be an enemy. And if this happens, vampires will be a prime target. People who only come out at night? That'll be seen as suspicious."

"You have a point," Mel said. "But if this war happens, the Vatican could be crippled. That means no more Redeemers hunting us."

He had the upper hand here, and he wasn't afraid to leverage that. "Yes, but *everyone* could begin hunting you. You probably don't believe in Hell, but that's what the world will become if Kyrios has his way." He didn't know if *he* still believed in Hell, but he figured it was good imagery to use. His faith was currently frail like a spider's web.

Mel shrugged. "Fair enough. But how do I know if any of this is true? How do I know you and that Brit didn't make it up? I need to know the person behind the story. Tell me about yourself."

"Not a whole lot to tell. I grew up in a super Christian family. We've all been, you know, active in our church. In fact, I came here for a Christianity conference. My friends were butchered because of that."

"Whoa, whoa, hold up," Mel said. "Are you talking about the hotel murders?"

"Yes," he said, choking up.

"And the same people who did that are planning on igniting a holy war?"

"That's right."

Mel seemed to mull it over for a minute. "The murders are a fact. Plus, there's the British woman's predictions. We suspected other vamps were involved, but we didn't know for sure. Jaz, have you confirmed this kid is a survivor of the attack?"

Jazmine replied, "The news said he's unaccounted for. Plus, that Redeemer damn sure believed it."

"All right, then. Kid, I guess your story checks out. What do you think, Jaz? Should we help them?"

"You know I do."

"Okay. Kid, we're in. And for what it's worth, I'm sorry for what you went through." Kyle didn't bother pointing out that he was *still* going through it, and in fact, had no idea when it would end.

His friends lying in pieces in that hotel room.

"Thanks, Mel. We appreciate that," he said.

"You can use our loft for the time being," she replied.

"And you can work at the bar in your spare time. I'll pay you," Jazmine added.

So, they had shelter and a source of income. God had definitely provided tonight. But if they were going to pose a real threat to Kyrios, they needed more manpower.

Someone tapped him on the shoulder. It was Chloe. "Come."

* * *

She took him to the last place he expected: a video store in the Bronx. "There are still video stores?" Kyle said, amazed.

"Name."

"Oh." The name of the store was The Last Action Video Store. "I had no idea there was still one left."

They went inside whereupon Kyle was hit by a blast of nostalgia. There were dozens of shelves filled with DVDs and Blu-rays. Other shelves were inhabited by video games. There were even freaking VHS tapes for sale. Meanwhile, posters of movies starring Schwarzenegger, Stallone, Chuck Norris, Bruce Lee, Jean-Claude Van Damme, Carl Weathers, and even Charles Bronson were plastered on the walls. There was even an old CRT TV hanging from the ceiling and playing an action movie he didn't recognize.

"This is cool, but why are we here?"

"Chloe! Welcome back!" A chiseled young Asian man came jaunting over. He had short, slick black hair and wore a tight-fitting white muscle shirt which showed off his pecs. He wouldn't have looked out of place at the gym. "Oh! You brought a friend!" He extended a hand, which Kyle shook. The man shook his hand heartily up and down. "Shaun Mifune, at your service!"

"Uh... hi." Kyle looked questioningly at Chloe.

"Here... for... him."

It would have been a lot easier if she had written a note explaining what they wanted with this guy. "Oh? You're here for me? I'm flattered. Come! Let me give you the grand tour."

He led them from aisle to aisle. "Here's action—our specialty. Here's sci-fi. Here's drama. Here's sports. Oh, and here's anime which is like my second favorite." Kyle had never cared for anime. Its frequent fan service and violence clashed with his Christian values.

He decided against voicing this, so, instead, he said, "Oh, you're Japanese?"

"From... Tokyo."

"Na, na, na, I told you, Chloe baby, I'm from Yokohama. A little farther south." Throughout this conversation, his hands were gesticulating enthusiastically. Everything he said was punctuated by a hand motion.

"Show... Kyle... ungh... back."

"Ohhhhhh, you want to see the Stash? Right this way!"

They followed him into the back office which Kyle saw, to his amazement, was filled with Eastern weapons. Swords, nun-chucks, sais; if a Ninja Turtle needed it, it could be found in here hanging on the walls. "Whoa! Are these real?"

"One hundred and twenty percent! Chloe can tell you. That's how we met. Her employer found out about the Stash, and they wanted to buy it from me. But this stuff is sacred! *Boku no isan!* You don't sell that."

"Wait, so Kyrios wanted these weapons? Did he happen to tell you what for?"

"No, and that made it even easier to turn him down. It all seemed real sketchy. The funny thing is, he wasn't pissed when I rejected his offer. I gathered he had only come here at Chloe's suggestion."

"You... showed... me."

"Yeah, it's my bad for letting you in on the Stash." He kept saying "the Stash" like it was the newest, hottest thing. He would have made a great copywriter. "But I don't regret it. Nothing bad happened, so it's all good."

Kyle and Chloe exchanged a worried look. "Actually, it's not." He wanted to confirm something before he continued. Indicating Shaun, he said, "Is he, you know...?" Kyle pointed to his fangs.

"Yes, I'm a vampire."

"Okay, cool. I just wanted to make sure I didn't look like an idiot here."

He grinned. "All idiots are welcome here at The Last Action Video Store."

"I think I get why we're here now," Kyle said.

"Recruit."

Shaun raised an eyebrow. "Recruit? For what?"

Kyle explained the situation to him. He could recite it by heart now.

Shaun's eyes went wild. "What the hell? Are you serious?"

"Yes," Chloe said.

"But a holy war? That's... I mean, you can't..."

"It's for real," Kyle said. "And if we don't stop it, millions, maybe even billions, could die."

Shaun put his game face on. "Okay, I'm in."

Kyle almost jumped back, as shocked as he was. "What? Just like that?"

"I'm descended from samurai. My ancestors fought the Mongolian invasion at Tsushima. I've always felt it was my destiny to be a defender. It all makes sense now."

"All right, well, um, welcome aboard."

"So, what's the plan, Shiro?"

"'Shiro'?"

Shaun laughed. "I just picked that name out for you. The Japanese word for white is *shiroi,* and you're pretty white, so I'll call you Shiro."

Just great. Now, in addition to being Sour Cream, he was also Shiro. That was fine, he supposed, if it would help stop Kyrios. But afterward, he would have to negotiate new nicknames. "You can call me whatever you want. The plan doesn't actually exist yet. Come by Marvelous Mel's on Greenwich tomorrow night. Ask for Jazmine. We'll have a strategy session to figure this out."

Shaun gave him a two-finger salute. "Will do, Shiro!"

December 8.

The next day, Angelica was holed up in bed in her room at the Holy See. The modifications the Vatican had made to her body allowed her to push herself farther than ordinary humans. However, she had gotten precious little sleep this week and the nanites in her bloodstream were overtaxed. Thus, she would have to rest today. The *fwoom-fwoom-fwoom* of the ceiling fan and frequent honking of cars outside were her only company at the moment.

The events of last night returned to her. Sure enough, the two deceased had been undead, and the injured officers had attested to seeing what were mostly likely Kyle Falconer and the albino in an adjacent alley. The suspects had roughed them up and there were a few broken bones, but no fatalities. She didn't understand. If she was correct in her belief they had killed the two vampires in the hotel, then why would they spare the policemen?

It was almost as if they had a code of ethics, which sounded ridiculous any way you looked at it. She had been to enough vampiric crime scenes to know their kind did what they wanted to *whom* they wanted, and they didn't let morality get in the way. And why should they? They were doomed to eternal hellfire by the mere act of being vampires, so what did they have to gain by being merciful?

Her phone chimed. She reached over to the table next to her bed and fumbled around for it. After finding it, she discovered she had gotten an encrypted text from the police. Turns out a supposedly abandoned meat plant in the city had been using a lot of electricity recently according to power company records she had asked them to acquire.

She smiled. Vampires needed shelter even more than humans, so of course, they would seek out abandoned buildings to inhabit. But her smile evaporated when she remembered she was in no condition to investigate right now. She would have to go at night. If there were undead in that plant, they would be awake when she arrived. The thought briefly crossed her mind to go tomorrow, but she rejected it. Time was of the essence, and every second lost brought the prophecy closer to coming true. The Vatican had been waiting, terrified, for 103 years. She would bring relief to them as soon as possible or die trying.

Luckily, her combat uniform was now ready to be deployed. The vampires would find her a stern test.

* * *

That night, Shaun arrived at the bar. Kyle and Chloe introduced him to Jazmine and Mel. "Nice to meet you, ladies!" he said, bowing. "It's been one beautiful woman after another since I met Chloe."

"Don't get any ideas, Romeo," Jazmine said.

"Oh, I don't know. He has a certain energetic charm," Mel said.

"I have come here to lend my assistance to your righteous cause," Shaun said.

"Are you really willing to risk your life for this?" Jazmine said, her arms crossed behind the bar.

"Sure! I come from a long line of protectors. It is my duty to assist you. And, let's be honest: A world without movies would bum me out too much."

The team gathered around the kitchen table in Jazmine and Mel's loft.

"Do we have a plan yet?" Shaun said.

Kyle replied, "Okay, so I met with Chloe in Alsakina earlier because that's one of the few ways we can carry on a conversation. She doesn't know when the Grand Imam will be arriving, only that it's soon. She does, however, know where the manzil has been hiding out. It's an abandoned plant in the Meatpacking District. That's our best chance of finding information."

"You suggesting we knock on their door and ask politely?" Jazmine said.

Kyle shook his head. "No. I'm suggesting we scope it out. And I'm suggesting we do it tonight."

"That's crazy!" Mel said. "We haven't had any time to prepare."

"I'm with them," Shaun said.

Kyle needed to convince them. "I understand your hesitation, but we don't know how much time we have. We need to make every second count. The Grand Imam could arrive tomorrow. The sooner we can gather information, the sooner we can come up with a more concrete plan."

"Concur."

"You're not wrong," Jazmine said. "But we don't have an idea of what we're up against."

Kyle replied, "Actually, we do. Chloe lived with them for most of her life. She knows them well. They're a tight-knit group, but they're small. She has since left, and we killed two of them two nights ago. That only leaves Kyrios, a French woman named Amelie, a Spaniard named Cortez, and six other Muslims Kyrios recruited during the Crusades. We have nine enemies to deal with, and there are five of us, so the odds aren't *too* bad."

"What are their Satanic Gifts?" Shaun asked.

Chloe shrugged. Kyle said, "Aside from Kyrios and the two we killed, we don't know. Kyrios has kept them a closely guarded secret. But I'm told Satanic Gifts never repeat, so I can tell you no one in the manzil is a shapeshifter and no one can cause vertigo. And Kyrios' Gift only affects the people he's turned, so it won't work on the rest of you."

"That doesn't narrow it down a whole lot," Mel said.

"That's why we need to gather intel," Kyle insisted.

Jazmine and Mel exchanged glances. Mel then said, "Fine. We can do it tonight. On one condition."

"What's that?"

"We see any sign of trouble, we get the hell out of there," Jazmine said.

Kyle shrugged. "Fair enough. What do you think, Shaun?"

He gave them double thumbs up. "Works for me."

"Okay. Let's get over there," Kyle said.

13

Kyle and Chloe stood in the parking lot of the meatpacking plant. It had long since been cleared of vehicles and now innumerable weeds had shot up through the cracks in the pavement. The building itself was completely dark with no lights on. "That doesn't mean anything," Jazmine had said when they first arrived. "Our kind can see in the dark, though not as well as with the lights on."

She, Mel, and Shaun had gone around to the rear of the building so that they could have two points of entry. Chloe had revealed there was a fire escape in the back they could use to gain access to the higher floors. She and Kyle would enter on the ground floor. This way, they could hopefully avoid a complete ambush.

Each of them was carrying a walkie-talkie. They had managed to get a set at Goodwill. It wasn't exactly high-tech but they would make do. Kyle's squawked. "We're in position," Mel said.

Kyle and Chloe approached the large doors of the entrance. "So are we. The doors are wide open."

"Not a good sign," Mel replied.

"Suspicious," Chloe added.

They walked through the doors, ears and eyes primed to spot trouble. The first floor of the plant was filled with abandoned equipment, although there was an open area with furniture in it. Kyle spoke softly into the walkie-talkie. "We're in. First floor's empty except for us."

"We made it in, too. We're in a hallway. There are no signs of life thus far. I mean, no signs of undead. Be careful, though; they could be using Thief in the Night."

Kyle and Chloe went over to the area with the furniture. It was in a corner. "Common... area," Chloe said.

There was a small, round table made of wood in the center. There were papers on it, but he didn't know if any of them would be useful. Only one way to find out. He began going through them. There was a note from Chloe saying she was abandoning Kyrios. "Wait, you had already made up your mind?"

"Not... me. Collins."

It made sense now. The Russian and the Irishman had made her out to be a traitor so they would be free to kill her and Kyle. Ironically, it made her turn her back on them for real.

The rest of the papers were newspaper clippings about the atrocities the manzil had carried out. Had they been planning on making a macabre scrapbook?

The stairs behind Kyle creaked. Chloe yelled, "Look...!"

He whirled around just in time for something sharp to slam into his shoulder. The impact hurled him into the wall next to Chloe. He found himself stuck to it, a sharp pain lancing through him.

"...out!"

Chloe hurled a pair of electric knives at a figure in a black suit emerging from the stairs. The mystery assailant put up an arm to block them. The knives lodged in it and the blue electricity spread throughout the attacker's body. "So, you're the one with the lightning Satanic Gift. I came prepared for you." It was the Redeemer, only now she wore a form-fitting black cat suit with what looked like night vision goggles over her eyes. Incredibly, she was completely unharmed by Chloe's attack.

Chloe readied another volley, but the Redeemer didn't give her a chance to use it. She was carrying a crossbow and she fired a long metal spike at Chloe. The latter was forced to contort herself backward as if playing a deadly game of limbo. The spike barely missed her, although she lost her grip on her knives and they flew up at the ceiling. There was a thunderous boom as they hit their unintended target. Dust and other minute particles came down on them.

Chloe managed to right herself, but by that point, the Redeemer was already in Kyle's face with the crossbow. She flipped up her goggles. "Make a move and he dies." Chloe stared angrily at her but did nothing else.

The walkie-talkie squawked. "What was that?" came Mel's voice.

"Tell her everything's fine," the Redeemer ordered Chloe.

Chloe picked it up. "False... alarm. Scared... by... ungh... shadow."

"Kyle? Are you okay?" Mel said.

He managed to get himself under control which wasn't easy with the amount of pain he was in. "I'm fine. Chloe just got jumpy."

"Okay, well, be careful. We don't want anyone to hear us."

"R-Roger," Kyle said.

The conversation over, the Redeemer turned to address Kyle. "I told you I would kill you next time we met. But first, I have questions."

He rolled his eyes dramatically. "What else is new?"

She leveled the crossbow at his crotch. "I have excellent aim. I can send you to Hell quickly or I can bring Hell to you. Your call."

"All right, fine. No sense holding back, I guess. You caught me."

Chloe continued to glare at her. This did not escape her notice. "Don't give me that look, monster. What we do is a blessing."

"Murder," Chloe shot back.

"Tell that to all the Redeemers. Most of them were orphaned by your kind." She turned her attention back to Kyle. "Who was Martha Shipton?"

"Who?"

"The woman in the church. Who was she?"

Kyle sighed. It couldn't hurt to answer now that the woman in question was dead. "Her name was Ursula Southeil. At least, that was what she told me."

She smiled with satisfaction. "Ah, now it makes sense. *Mother* Shipton was a vampire. That explains her unholy ability to predict the future.

"Next question. Did you kill the vampires in the Midtown apartment?"

"Yes. But that was self-defense. They tried to kill us first."

"Why did you spare the police officers who tried to detain you?"

That seemed like a silly question to Kyle. "They weren't trying to kill *us*. Why would we kill *them?*"

"Fine, fine," she said. "I'll pretend you have a moral compass. How is the Siren Sisterhood involved with this?"

"The what?"

She frowned. "Never mind. I can see by your expression she never bothered to tell you about it. You don't need to know, anyway."

Kyle was intrigued. What was this Siren Sisterhood and what did it have to do with Ursula? He knew he should have been scared to death at the situation he was in, but he saw it as a chance to establish a dialogue. "We're not your enemies."

"Silence! Next question. Who's in charge of your manzil?"

"We don't exactly have a manzil. We barely even know each other. The person you want is Kyrios. He's the leader of the vampire gang in New York."

It was almost imperceptible, but she raised an eyebrow slightly. "And where can I find this Kyrios?"

Kyle explained, "This was his most recent base of operations."

"And he left you here to guard it while he's away?"

Kyle shook his head violently, amplifying the pain in his shoulder. "No! We're not with him. We want to stop him from igniting a holy war."

"Enough lies!"

The ceiling above them collapsed. It was going to fall on the Redeemer. He didn't have time to think about the pain. He focused all his energy on breaking free of the spike that had pinned him to the wall. With a roar, he exploded loose and shoved her out of the way.

Hundreds of pounds of rubble slammed down on him. He groaned as every part of him took a beating. Internal bleeding was not out of the question.

"Kyle!" Chloe said. She hurried to lift the pieces of concrete off him.

The Redeemer got up and stared dumbfounded at him. "Why did you save me?"

Within moments, the rubble was clear and Kyle sat with his back against it. The pain had subsided to a dull ache. Everywhere. "I told you. We're not your enemies. We're trying to stop a holy war. We came here tonight to find information that will help us do that."

Jazmine, Mell, and Shaun came running down the stairs. The Redeemer pivoted and leveled her crossbow at them. The trio assumed defensive postures. The Redeemer's gaze fell upon Jazmine. "You!"

"Stop! Stop! Everyone, stop! This is a huge misunderstanding!" Kyle said.

Chloe got between the Redeemer and the trio, putting her hands out to indicate both sides should keep their cool. Reluctantly, all four of them stood down.

"Why is there a Redeemer here?" Mel said.

"She's the one I told you about," Jazmine said.

"To answer your question, I came here to kill vampires."

"No shit," Mel shot back.

"I told you we should have brought Shaun's weapons," Jazmine said.

"You guys need training," Shaun said and began fidgeting. "*Minna wa jouzu ja nai!*"

"*Watashi wa totemo jouzu desu yo,*" the Redeemer said. "*Kantan ni anata wo korosu koto ga dekiru, bakemono.*"

Shaun was agape. "You speak Japanese?"

"I speak many languages. It helps me get closer to my prey."

"Listen!" Kyle said. "I think introductions are in order. I'm Kyle, that's Chloe, and they're Jazmine, Mel, and Shaun."

Jazmine and Mel continued to glare at the Redeemer. Shaun waved sheepishly at her.

The vampire hunter's eyes went back and forth between them. Finally, she said, "Angelica Brassi."

"What?" Kyle said.

She turned to face him. "My name is Angelica Brassi. I don't know why I'm telling you this. Maybe I'm just using you to get to the root of the problem."

"Fair enough," Kyle said.

"Now, tell me about this holy war."

Here we go again. Kyle explained it to her.

Angelica was silent for a moment. Finally, "This Kyrios is the one who must be stopped, then." Kyle was glad he was no longer included in that.

"Yes. He's behind all the recent murders in the city. And we could use some help stopping him."

"Hmph. Forget it. You are my enemies. I would never work with you. But, if I happened to receive intelligence from an anonymous source, I would be free to act on it."

Kyle nodded. "I get you. And where could one send that intelligence?"

Angelica just happened to say aloud her cell phone number. Kyle just happened to commit it to memory.

"Okay," he said. "We don't know you and this conversation never happened. Unfortunately, we also don't know when the Grand Imam will arrive."

"December 14th," Angelica said matter-of-factly.

"Seriously? You know when he's coming?" Shaun said.

Angelica turned around to address him. "We are well connected. The Vatican keeps a close eye on other religious figures."

Kyle managed to get back to his feet and ripped the spike out of his shoulder. A laser beam of pain shot through him. "Gah! But that's great. You can warn him. He doesn't come and the war is averted."

"Perhaps," Angelica said. "But this Kyrios doesn't sound like the type to give up easily. He'll keep trying until he succeeds. And next time, we might not be able to anticipate his plan. It would be better to set a trap and catch him in it. That way, we could remove the threat once and for all."

But Jazmine said, "That's a bad idea. If we fuck it up, the war will happen. They bombed a train station for far less. Who knows what they'll do if the Grand Imam is killed."

"Which is why I'm not leaving it to you. We'll handle this," Angelica said.

"You need our help," Kyle insisted.

"You said you needed *my* help," Angelica said.

"We can help *each other,*" Mel said.

"Nothing personal, but there is still time to warn the Grand Imam," Shaun said.

"Thank you, but this is my call. I say the Grand Imam will not be warned," Angelica said.

Jazmine and Mel glared at her. "I say we go over her head and warn him ourselves," Jazmine said.

Angelica laughed. "And how would you verify the veracity of your claims? You would be immediately dismissed. But us? We are the Vatican. We are authority itself. You cannot stop God."

"Why... looked... ungh... scared?"

"Excuse me?" Angelica said.

"She's right," Kyle said. "You do look scared. But why would that be if God is on your side?"

Angelica stared at the floor for a moment. "There is a prophecy."

Kyle hadn't been expecting that answer. "A prophecy?"

Angelica explained, "In 1917, a series of prophecies was made by the Madonna at Fatima, Portugal."

"I've heard about those. One prophecy foretold the end of World War I, one predicted the consecration of Russia, and the third predicted the attempted assassination of Pope John Paul II," Kyle said.

Angelica shook her head. "The third one was a lie because the truth was too horrific to disclose. It actually states unholy abominations will bring about the destruction of the world. The Church, along with select ally nations, initiated the Fatima Protocol to stop the prophecy from coming true. That is one reason we Redeemers are trained."

"So, what happens if the prophecy is thwarted? Will you Redeemers go away?" Shaun said.

"Don't press your luck," Angelica said. "Only one part of our mission is to stop the prophecy from happening. We will exist as long as vampires do."

"No... peace?"

"No. Your group might be inoffensive, but can you say the same for all the other manzils?"

"But we're not..." Kyle started to say. "Never mind." They were not a manzil, though. "We should be getting back."

"Can we trust this bitch not to follow us?" Jazmine said.

"I'll thank you to keep your crude opinions to yourself."

"It's fine. I think we have an understanding," Kyle said.

"Only with me, and not officially," Angelica said. "Any other Redeemer you encounter will kill you on sight."

"Good to know," Mel said sarcastically.

"I was merely granting you the courtesy of a warning."

Kyle decided to get the conversation back on track. "Where will the Grand Imam touch down in New York?"

"John F. Kennedy International Airport," Angelica said. "The gate has not yet been assigned. Know that security will be at maximum level."

"Not... maximum. Enough."

Kyle concurred. "Chloe's right. The Grand Imam may be protected against human threats, but they've never faced this before."

"Rest assured, I will be there as well. And I *have* faced this threat many times. But if you're still not satisfied, I will also request reinforcements from the Vatican." She said the last line sarcastically, indicating their satisfaction was not a concern.

"Good enough," Kyle said. "And when you find out the gate number, you can 'accidentally' release it to a random number which I will give you. We still need to buy some burner phones."

"Accidents do happen," Angelica replied. Kyle couldn't tell if she was joking.

* * *

They returned to Jazmine and Mel's loft where they once again gathered in the kitchen area. "I don't trust her," Mel said.

"Me, neither," Jazmine added.

"She's not a bad person. If she was, she would have killed me when she had the chance," Kyle said.

"She's probably suckering us in so she and her buddies can wipe us all out at once," Mel said.

"Or, maybe she rightly sees the Kyrios manzil as the greater threat and is desperate to stop the holy war," Shaun suggested.

"Whatever," Jazmine said. "We can go along with her, but if anything happens, I'm holding you white people responsible."

"I'm not white," Shaun said.

"Whatever, you're white enough to blame if this goes south," Jazmine said with just the faintest smile. Shaun just shook his head with good humor.

"Okay, look," Kyle said. "The Grand Imam arrives on the 14th. That's in five days. We don't have much time to prepare. Shaun, can you train us to use those weapons?"

"Of course, I can. Just leave it to me! Come on by tomorrow."

"We'll be there," Kyle said.

"All right, I need to get back. The sun's coming up soon and my store isn't going to close itself," Shaun said.

"You didn't close it when you came over?" Kyle said.

Shaun shrugged. "I may have gotten a little too excited to get over here and have our first strategy session."

"Yes, you should probably get back there before someone steals all your VHS tapes and sells them on the black market," Jazmine said.

"I know you're joking, but that's exactly what I'll do." And with that, they all laughed and he left.

14

Angelica typed up her report and sent it to the Vatican.

(Translated from Italian)

"I have ascertained the plans of the unholy monsters in this city. They plan to assassinate the Grand Imam when he arrives, thus initiating a holy war that will ravage the world. I am hereby requesting reinforcements to guard the Grand Imam when he arrives. This will have the dual benefit of not only ensuring his well-being and thwarting the prophecy, but it will also show solidarity between our two faiths.

"In addition, I have confirmed the survival (perhaps 'continued existence' would be a better term) of Kyle Falconer. However, he has been turned (though firmly against his will) and can no longer be counted on the side of God. I do not know his location, but I feel it would be best not to tell Eve about this. The knowledge that her brother is now an undead abomination would weigh on her heavily and hinder her work to strengthen unity across denominations. Cruel though it may be, she must believe Kyle was killed in the massacre. I will arrange for the police to issue a statement to the effect they have identified his remains among the victims. No one will ever find out our deception.

"I look forward to ending this threat and will be awaiting further instructions.

"Yours in Christ. Angelica."

* * *

December 9.

The next night, Kyle, Chloe, Jazmine, and Mel went over to Last Action Video Store. They were expecting Shaun's cheery self, but when they went inside, they found him pacing and ranting angrily in Japanese in the midst of a trashed store. Shelves had been pushed over and videos lay everywhere. They awkwardly stepped over them.

"What's going on?" Kyle asked him.

"Yaro!" Shaun yelled. *"Karera wa boku no buki o nusunda!"*

"English!" Mel said.

"Sorry," he said. "I slip back into Japanese when I'm stressed. They took the weapons."

"Who's 'they'?" Jazmine said.

"Jigoku no Jimusho," Shaun said. "Hell's Office. They're undead Yakuza. Not the sort of people you want to mess with."

"Well, why are they messing with *you?*" Jazmine said.

"Well... I sort of stole from them."

They gaped at him. "You what?"

"I stole the weapons from them because *they* had stolen them in the first place. See, they aren't just weapons; they're antiques that date back hundreds of years. The Office were going to sell them on the black market. But that's our heritage! They belong in a museum."

Jazmine pinched her nose in frustration. "So, then, *why* did you keep them in your store?"

"Well..."

"We're waiting," Mel said.

He shrugged. "They're really cool."

Kyle sighed and shook his head. "If you had given them to a museum in the first place, this wouldn't have happened to you. I guess we'll just have to do without the weapons."

Shaun looked away sheepishly. "Well, it's not that simple. I'm marked now. They'll keep coming after me until they kill me. And anyone I'm associated with."

"Idiot," Chloe said.

Mel threw up her hands in exasperation. "Let's ditch this guy before we get caught up in his bullshit."

Shaun laughed nervously. "It's actually too late. See, they also stole my security tapes of the last week. They'll know who's been in here."

"Doesn't mean they'll be able to identify us. I say we get the hell out of here," Jazmine said.

The vampires of color turned to leave. But Kyle said, "Wait! We can't just abandon him. That's not what Jesus would have done."

"Fuck Jesus," Mel said. Kyle blushed at the blasphemy.

"I'm actually Shinto," Shaun said.

I'm trying to help you, dummy. "It doesn't matter what anyone's religious beliefs are. My conscience is telling me not to abandon Shaun."

"We didn't sign up for war with an undead triad," Jazmine said.

"Yakuza," Shaun corrected.

"Whatever! My point is, we've already got our hands full trying to save the world. We don't need this."

"Exactly," Kyle said. "We're trying to save the world. We can't afford to be a man down. We're going to need all the help we can get."

"I'd say you're trying to get us all the *enemies* we can get," Mel said.

But Kyle said, "Maybe we don't have to be enemies. Shaun, what would it take for the Office to forgive you?"

Shaun rubbed his chin thoughtfully. "Well, a finger would suffice for the regular Yakuza. But the Office would want a whole hand."

Kyrios' words echoed in Kyle's mind. *You understand now. You don't, but your body does. It recognizes me as a part of itself, like a limb. You can't kill me without being willing to cut off your own arm.* This gave him a grim idea. A hand would probably work just as well as an arm. He spent several long moments mulling it over. The idea was both appalling and terrifying, but it might also be their best shot.

"Kyle?" Chloe said, concern showing on her face.

Finally, Kyle said, "Shaun, arrange a meeting with the Office. I'll give them my hand."

"What?" they yelled.

"I mean it. If I can cut off a piece of my body, I should be able to overcome Kyrios' Satanic Gift."

Shaun stared dumbfounded at him. "Well... I mean... they probably won't care who's hand it is. But are you good with this?"

"Definitely not. But I think I have to do it. It's the best way to get through this."

"All right," Shaun said. "I don't exactly have their number, but I'll ask around Little Tokyo in East Village. Someone there should know. And Kyle?"

"Yes?"

"Thanks."

"Thank me after we get through this."

* * *

A colored soldier training ground. A Civil War prison camp. A mental asylum. A missile storage facility. A homeless shelter. A tuberculosis sanitarium. A drug treatment center. A cemetery. A planned amusement park. A boy's reformatory. A quarantine station.

Hart Island had been all of these things since New York began using it in 1864 during the Civil War. Located on Long Island Sound's western end as part of the Bronx, it was perhaps best known as a resting place of more than a million people. But now it was Kyrios' final base of operations.

The manzil stood around him in the open reception room of one of the dilapidated buildings on the island. They were all wearing their robes. "The meat-packing plant has been discovered," Amelie said.

He shrugged. "It doesn't matter. We left no clues about where we were headed. And no one lives on this island."

"Has that pisswipe actually turned against us?" Cortez said angrily. His brown skin meshed well with his buzzed hair.

"Forget about her," Kyrios said. "She's *maleun* and was never truly one of us. She was an expendable pawn who obeyed out of fear rather than ideology. If she attacks us, we will kill her."

"If *those two* hadn't betrayed us as well, Kyle Falconer would have one less ally on his side, and we would be at full strength," Ahmad said. He was the tallest among them at six-foot-five as well as one of the six Muslims Kyrios had recruited during the First

Crusade. The others were Basheer, Faysal, Imad, Naeem, and Irfan. Nobody bothered to point out the fact Kyle Falconer had also lost an ally in Ursula Southeil.

Kyrios replied, "Consider it a culling. The unfaithful have been naturally excised. I'm not a strict believer in survival of the fittest—I find it distracts me from the real people that must be eliminated—but it has proven sound this week."

"However, Mikhail set his own plot to kill the Grand Imam into action," Amelie said.

"Hmph. His plan is an anonymous text message. Ours is a broadcast. The entire Christian world will know who brought about their destruction. The weak links have been severed. Our collective will is now ironclad.

"Lutherans; Presbyterians; Church of Christ; Protestants. It makes no difference. I chose the Catholic Church as the face of our enemy because it launched the Crusades, but they all must die."

They all knelt before him, chanting, "Born in the blood of Christ, we now destroy him."

And in a few days, they would do exactly that.

* * *

"Are you sure about this?" Chloe said. They had gone to Alsakina to talk. They currently sat on the bed in Chloe's childhood bedroom.

"If you're asking if I like the idea—no. But it makes the most sense out of all possible plans. It's much better to make a peace offering to the Office rather than go to war with them *and* Kyrios. Besides, we don't have time to fight them anyway. We need to focus on stopping the holy war. Then, there's the fact neither of us can attack Kyrios unless we're willing to cut off a chunk of our own body. I can't ask the others to fight in my place, and I can't ask you to give your hand for me."

"You're already willing. Do you have to go all the way with it?"

"To be honest, I won't know if I'm truly willing unless I actually do it. I need to know before I take on Kyrios."

Chloe smiled. "I knew you were strong, Kyle, but I never expected you to do this. It's so brave of you."

Kyle stared at his hands. "I don't even know which one they'll take. I keep wondering what it will feel like."

"Don't," she said. "There's no need to torture yourself further."

"Heh. Worrying's a funny thing. I don't want to, but some part of me feels like I won't be prepared if I don't."

"Kyle, nothing can prepare you for something like this. Having witnessed extreme violence many times, I can tell you to make it quick. One quick slice." Her voice lowered. "That's what I always did when I had to kill for them." She looked away.

Kyle thought it would help to talk about it. It wasn't like the manzil would have heard her complaints. "If you don't mind my asking, how did you deal with it?" She was silent. "I'm sorry; I shouldn't have asked."

"No, it's fine. Over the past fifty years, there have been many unsolved murders in New York. We're probably responsible for half of them. I was never spared; Kyrios mandated each member had to participate in the slaughter. I tried to kill from behind so I wouldn't have to look into my victims' eyes, but sometimes I had to attack from the front.

The times I forgot to look away are the times that haunt me the most. I saw the fear in their eyes, the shock when they realized they were going to die. That they were going to leave this world for somewhere completely unknown."

A question had been eating away at him for a while now. He didn't want to ask, but he couldn't hold back anymore. "You said every member had to kill. My college group. Did you...?"

She looked away. "Yes, I did. I can tell you who it was if you want. At least, I can describe the person."

He grimaced. "No, that's fine. I don't think I want to know."

"Oh." She sounded almost disappointed, as if she wanted to get it off her chest.

He now wanted to be on any subject except this one. "Do you believe in an afterlife?"

She shrugged. "My parents did. Even Kyrios believes in God. You got his blood, so you should have seen the things he saw. Christ was real. I think the better question is, is the afterlife a place any of us actually want to go to?"

"I always believed it was," Kyle said. "I was taught Heaven was the ultimate paradise where you can never be unhappy."

"And why is that, Kyle? With the sheer variety of people in this world, surely someone would find Heaven not to their liking. Or does God mind-control everyone into being happy? That doesn't sound particularly appealing to me."

"Better than going to Hell," Kyle said.

He instantly regretted his quip when she replied, "I'm going there anyway."

"Don't say that! God forgives as long as you repent, and you've done that."

She shook her head slightly. "Surely, you've read the Old Testament. You know the Judeo-Christian god is a vengeful one. Besides, we're unholy creatures of the night now. There's no forgiveness for us."

Kyle didn't fully understand why he said what he said next. Perhaps it was an impulsive reaction to make her feel better. "Someday, I'll find God and make him forgive you."

She locked eyes with him. "You mean it, Kyle? Do you promise?"

He had said it, and since it seemed to have perked her up, he couldn't take it back. "Yes, Chloe. I promise."

She hugged him. "Thank you so much! I never dared to hope... I always thought I was doomed."

Having a chat with God was a tall order. He knew that. But he wasn't about to let her down. Her happiness depended on this. Maybe she was willing to latch onto any lifeline she could find, but it now went without saying her hopes lay in him confronting the Almighty.

✳ ✳ ✳

December 10.

As it turned out, Shaun had a van. He was the only one of them with a vehicle, so they piled into it the next night to head to the meeting with Hell's Office. The appearance of the van itself was impressive; the robot from the 1927 German silent film *Metropolis* was airbrushed onto the side. "I love the original," he said. "Although the Osamu Tezuka version was great, too."

Now, they were driving to the spot. Shaun insisted on giving everyone a Yakuza crash course. "The Yakuza are organized into a pyramid hierarchy. You've got the *oyabun*, he's the boss and the father figure. The guys below him are the *kobun*, his children, in effect. The organization is basically a family.

"The mortal Yakuza use a ritual called *yubizume,* or finger shortening, when a member breaks their code. Hell's Office is more hardcore; their ritual is *udezume*—arm shortening. Instead of your finger, you give a hand."

"Great," Kyle said without a hint of enthusiasm. It was taking all his willpower to avoid visibly trembling.

"Be sure to bow when you meet them. Respect is everything to them. Speak only when spoken to. And don't worry about bleeding out; your vampire regeneration will cauterize the wound within moments."

"Is it too late to back out?" Mel said. She and Jazmine sat in the second row in front of Kyle and Chloe.

"Very much so. If we back out now, they'll just get that much more insulted and bloodthirsty. You don't waste their time."

"Except when it comes to stealing their shit," Jazmine said.

"I'm sorry! I wasn't thinking. I just didn't want them to sell those weapons on the black market."

"Let's just get through this," Kyle said. The closer they got to the meeting point, the calmer he became. After all, it wasn't like he was going to die tonight—he hoped. Just a little off the top, right? It was basically a haircut, but an arm cut instead. *I might be going crazy here.*

Their journey ended up taking them across the Brooklyn Bridge into Brooklyn proper, at which point Shaun began driving southwest. Eventually, they arrived at their destination.

"Here we are," he said.

"And where exactly is here?" Kyle said.

"Brooklyn Bridge Park—Pier 6."

"We're meeting at a pier?" Jazmine said.

Shaun shook his head. "Not exactly. We're meeting them on their yacht."

"They have a yacht? Nice," Mel said.

"Fancy," Chloe added.

Shaun parked the van along the side of the street and they began walking up the pier. To their right was one of those golf places with the big net walls where you could hit all the balls you wanted. To their left was the biggest privately-owned boat anyone had ever seen. It looked to them like a miniature cruise ship. It had at least ten levels and even a helicopter on top. It had to have been two-hundred feet long at least. Along the side in big letters were the characters "流れ星."

"What does that say?" Mel said.

"*Nagareboshi,*" Shaun replied. "It means shooting star."

"Such a whimsical name for a boat owned by thugs," Jazmine said.

"Quiet! They have excellent hearing," Shaun said.

At the rear of the yacht was a ramp leading down to the pier. A Japanese man in a fancy suit met them in front of it. *"Osaki ni douzo,"* he said, gesturing up the ramp.

"He says to go on up," Shaun said.

They did so and were soon on the deck of the yacht itself. Kyle couldn't help but be impressed despite the grim circumstances which had brought them here.

The man who had given them the go-ahead to come on up followed them. The crew of the yacht (who were probably not Yakuza based on their decidedly inferior attire) began bringing up the ramp.

Another Japanese man in a sharp suit and glasses came over to meet them. "Hello. I am Yoshikazu. Thank you for coming. Follow me, please."

He turned around to lead them, but the ramp man said, "*Chotto matte.*"

Yoshikazu replied, "*Nani?*"

The ramp man pointed to Jazmine. "*Ano onna wa watashitachi wo bujoku shimashita. Kanojo wa watashitachi wo kyōaku-han to yonda!*"

"*Sou ka,*" Yoshikazu said. He turned to address them. "He says this one called us thugs. You have further insulted us with this, Mifune-san."

Shaun put his hands together as if in prayer. "Please forgive them! They know nothing of our culture."

"Spare me your apologies. Udezume would have sufficed, but now a greater price must be paid."

This had somehow gone from horrific to even worse. Kyle was afraid they might not leave here alive, after all. His stomach seemed to tighten until it became the mass of a black hole. Would they be able to fight their way out? Perhaps, but then they'd be fully at war with Hell's Office. They all needed to keep a level head here. "What is the greater price?"

Yoshikazu explained, "We have an intricate system for meting out punishment. Each offense has an associated method of atonement. For stealing, it is udezume, and for insulting us, it is *meiyo kettou.*"

"What is meiyo kettou?" He asked, terrified of what the answer might be.

"Honor duel. One of you must face a designated opponent in combat. More specifically, you must face one of us who has accrued his own share of offenses. Right now, that would be Toshiyama. He's a rebellious one who needs to learn some humility."

"So, I win and you'll forgive us?"

"I'm afraid it is not that simple. As I said, each offense has a corresponding act of redemption. Winning the meiyo kettou only earns forgiveness of the insult. You would still need to commit udezume to forgive Mifune-san's transgression."

Kyle could feel his world crumbling once again. He didn't know if he was strong enough to do this. After all, how could anyone be expected to fight a duel *and* cut off their hand on the same night? It was too much.

Someone squeezed his hand. It was Chloe. "'You can do it, Kyle.'"

"Wait, how did you say that normally?" Mel asked.

It was then he noticed she was reading a sheet of paper in her other hand. "'I can speak just find when I'm reading something that's been pre-written for me.'"

Oh, so that was how she had been able to make her video speech as part of David's Purge. Kyle's resolve was strengthened by her continued belief in him. And it felt a-freaking-mazing having her hand in his—even if both their hands were ice-cold. And even if Kyle was about to lose his.

He turned back to face Yoshikazu. "All right, I'll do it. Bring on Toshiyama."

"Right this way," Yoshikazu said, and they followed him down into the depths of the yacht. He eventually brought them to a floor that strongly resembled a nightclub. There was a fully-stocked bar at the far end, a dance floor circle in the middle, to the right was a DJ booth, and to the left...

"That is a fucking shark tank!" Jazmine said. The whole left wall was a glass tank with bull sharks swimming about inside.

"Indeed," Yoshikazu said. "The shark, or *same,* is revered by us for its tenacity and fighting spirit. I hope that Falconer-san shows us the same attributes tonight." *Yeah, me too.*

There were about a dozen people, men and women, dancing on the dance floor, but Yoshikazu went over to the DJ booth and got him to turn the music off. He then announced over the mic, *"Minna, dansu furoa wo hanarete kudasai."*

And with that, everyone took up positions around the perimeter of the dance floor. An elderly Japanese man with thinning gray hair in a beige *yukata*, who had been sitting off to the side, stood up and approached the newcomers. "Is it time for the udezume?" he asked Yoshikazu.

"There is a bit of a complication. But first, everyone, this is our oyabun Sakazuki.

"Nice to meet you," Kyle said. It honestly wasn't, but what was he to say?

"What exactly is the complication, Yoshikazu?"

"They have insulted us and thus must carry out meiyo kettou."

"Ah," the old man said. He stood with a slight hunch. "Most unfortunate."

"Yes, oyabun. But I was thinking it is also an opportunity of redemption for Toshiyama. We could teach him some humility if he survives."

Kyle froze. "Did you say 'survive'?" Kyle said.

Yoshikazu nodded. "Yes. Meiyo kettou is a fight to the death."

Mel whispered in his ear, "We need to get the hell out of here."

Kyle looked at the mob which surrounded them. "A little late for that, I think." No, the only option was to fight one person and win rather than taking on the entire organization.

"Indeed," Sakazuki said, his arms crossed. "It would not bode well for you to insult us further by trying to escape."

"I'm just looking to get this over with," Kyle said. "Bring on my opponent."

"As you wish," Yoshikazu said. "Toshiyama! *Kitte! Kitte!*"

A door opened next to the bar and the biggest person Kyle had ever seen walked out. He had to have been at least seven feet tall and was built like an armored truck. He wore an expensive suit that was obviously tailored. In addition, he had long, wild black hair which came down to his shoulders.

"Christ," Jazmine said. Kyle shared her sentiment (with a bit less blasphemy) but again, the only way out was through this guy.

Toshiyama lumbered over to the dance floor and looked around with annoyance. "*Nani?*" His voice boomed with irritation.

Yoshikazu pointed at Kyle and said, "*Kare to* meiyo kettou *wo shite kudasai.*"

Toshiyama released a laugh that was heavy with bass while baring his fangs. "*Baka yarou.*"

Kyle felt he had just been insulted, but it was somewhat difficult to be angry at such a terrifying person. He was more scared than anything.

Yoshikazu explained, "The rules are simple. Each of you will be given a katana from the collection recently retrieved from Mifune-san. Kill your opponent, but fight with honor. No groin strikes or attacks to the eyes. And no Satanic Gift." That last one was good news to Kyle.

"No... hand," Chloe said, pointing to Toshiyama's right arm which ended in a stump.

"Ah, yes," Yoshikazu said. "As you can see, he has had more than one offense to atone for."

Toshiyama wouldn't be able to swing his sword with full force. Kyle wasn't likely to get any more advantages, but he would take this one.

An attendant came over and presented Kyle with a katana with a beautiful green hilt. He took it and the heft and danger of it struck him. He had the means to expedite an end to someone's life with this—and indeed, they expected him to.

The attendant presented Toshiyama with his sword which he eyed lustfully.

Both Kyle and Toshiyama advanced to meet each other on the dance floor circle. The latter removed his shirt to reveal an upper body absolutely slathered in tattoos. Kyle couldn't even keep up with everything going on artistically on his body. Dragons; demons; naked women; skulls; Toshiyama's torso had it all except for any trace of fat.

Everyone else backed away to the far corners of the room, giving them plenty of space. Evidently, Yoshikazu was going to act as a referee because he stayed with them. "On my mark, you will begin." Kyle tensed up, knowing that any moment the giant in front of him would try to kill him. He gripped his sword with both hands. *"Hajime!"*

15

Toshiyama swung his sword as if swinging a mountain. Kyle put his own sword up to block but was slammed backward. His katana went spinning away from him along the floor like a buzz saw. Several people jumped out of the way to avoid being sliced.

Toshiyama thundered forward and thrust his sword down towards Kyle's chest. Kyle kicked his leg out from under him, causing Toshiyama to stumble. The giant's katana was embedded in the floor mere inches from Kyle's shoulders. *Maybe that wasn't the best idea.*

In his desperation, Kyle tried to grab Toshiyama's sword, realizing too late the stupidity of that. His hand was sliced by the blade, and anyway, it was still stuck in the floor. Hot pain flared through his hand. His opponent laughed. *"Baka kuso."* Kyle didn't need a translator to know he had been insulted again.

Toshiyama effortlessly pulled his katana from the floor and prepared once again to turn Kyle into sashimi. With no time to lose, Kyle leapt and delivered a palm strike to his opponent's nose. There was a sickening crunch Kyle both heard and felt. Toshiyama roared and backed away from him.

Scrambling to his feet, Kyle looked all around the room to find his sword. He spotted it lying against the wall next to the stairs. He rushed over and picked it up. The massive gash on his hand was healing now, so he could just barely grip the hilt with both hands.

A roar behind him got his attention. He spun around just in time to duck a decapitating strike from Toshiyama. The big man was too close for an effective sword strike, so Kyle settled for kneeing him in the stomach. However, this proved to be a mistake as his opponent's abdomen was hard as steel. The highly resistible force met the immovable object. There was no give whatsoever. Toshiyama responded by backhanding him with the stump of his arm. Bright lights flashed in Kyle's eyes and he stumbled to get away.

Another roar sounded, but Kyle's vision hadn't recovered, and his brains were scrambled to a degree, so he dropped to his knees and rolled forward hoping to avoid whatever attack Toshiyama was launching. A frustrated yell from Toshiyama and a decided lack of Kyle being sliced up told him he was successful.

His vision then healed. Toshiyama stood in front of the stairs, his blade stuck in the wall. He yanked it out angrily and grunted with frustration. Fixing his gaze upon Kyle, he drove his sword ninety degrees vertically into the floor. *What's he up to?*

Toshiyama spread his good arm palm-first toward Kyle. There was a sense of electricity in the air. Something was coming.

"Dame da!" Yoshikazu yelled.

The room was then enveloped in all-consuming darkness which spread out from Toshiyama. The people inside murmured nervously.

"We said no Satanic Gifts!" Sakazuki reminded Toshiyama.

Kyle couldn't see a damn thing in this. He could hear just fine, but there wasn't a single speck of light left in the room.

"Falconer-san!" Yoshikazu said. "Since Toshiyama has violated the terms of this duel, you are free to use your Satanic Gift." Great. Except he didn't have one.

The situation was dead simple. Toshiyama had blacked out the room and was probably still inside it. That meant he could attack at any time and Kyle wouldn't see him coming.

Calm down. You need to focus. He closed his eyes and tried tuning out everything except his opponent. Toshiyama was a big guy and Kyle remembered how he stomped across the floor.

Thump.

Thump.

Thump.

The gargantuan Yakuza was lumbering toward him, chuckling all the while. But how close was he?

Thump.

He was only a few feet away. Kyle was sure of it. Should he wait for another step or should he strike now? Torturous indecision wracked him.

Kyle was struck with the sudden conviction he needed to attack *now*. Without any more delay, he swung his sword with both arms in a horizontal slash.

Toshiyama screamed and the darkness was sucked back into him. Kyle's eyes fell upon the bloody hand on the floor still gripping a katana. Toshiyama fell to his knees and Kyle pressed his blade to the side of his opponent's neck.

A visibly terrified Toshiyama blurted out, *"Boku wa koufuku shimasu!"*

"If that's your way of surrendering, I accept," he shot back.

"It is a fight to the death," Yoshikazu reminded him.

"You said to fight honorably," Kyle said. "It's not honorable to kill a man with no hands."

Sakazuki came forward. "I suppose it is your right as victor. Though Toshiyama-kun is shamed now."

Kyle didn't care. "You wanted him to learn humility. I'd say he just did."

The attendant from earlier ran over to assist Toshiyama with his wounds. The big man staggered over to the couch where Sakazuki had been sitting earlier.

Yoshikazu bowed to Kyle. "Well done employing the *Akuma no Chokkan*, Falconer-san."

"The what?"

"My apologies. Western vampires call it Devil's Intuition. You surely used it to defeat Toshiyama."

Kyle shrugged. "Is that a Satanic Gift?"

"Indeed," Sakazuki said. "It is very difficult to learn. If I may ask, how old are you?"

"I'm twenty-one. I was only recently turned."

Yoshikazu beamed. "You must have had an excellent teacher to learn Devil's Intuition at such a young age!"

Kyle's disposition dropped. "She actually didn't teach it to me. She died before she could."

"That is most unfortunate," Sakazuki said. "You have my sympathies."

"Just to be clear," Kyle said. "When I was in the dark, I suddenly knew with absolute certainty it was the time to strike. And that's Devil's Intuition?"

"Yes!" Yoshikazu said.

"It is a most difficult skill," Sakazuki reiterated.

Kyle had picked up a new Satanic Gift—and without Ursula to teach him. He became struck with a longing for her to be here to see this.

The others came over to congratulate him. "Well... done!"

"You did it!" Mel said.

"I think I may have underestimated you, Sour Cream."

"You beat a Yakuza, Shiro!"

"Uh, thanks," Kyle said. It was a bit too soon to celebrate, though.

As if in response to that thought, Sakazuki shifted the topic back to the reason they had come here in the first place. "Victory is well and good, but you still must answer for Mifune-san's crime."

Kyle tensed up again. "I'm ready."

The attendant cleaned Toshiyama's blood off the floor, and then they were ready to finally end this. A table, only about a foot high, was brought in, and a white cloth was placed over it. Yoshikazu gestured to Kyle, and he waited for the attendant to bring over something to cut his hand off with. It took him a few moments to realize the truth. *You're still holding your katana. They expect you to use that.*

As Kyle was right-handed, he decided to sacrifice his left one. With his heart beating a bombastic symphony in his chest, he grimly sat down at the table. He placed his left arm on the cloth and put the blade against his wrist. By this point, he was on the verge of hyper-ventilating. He could also feel his adrenaline starting to run out which he feared would affect his ability to numb the pain.

"'You can do it, Kyle,'" Chloe said again.

It was okay. Just rip the bandage off. Except this was one hell of a bandage to rip off. Still, her words had a calming effect on him. He closed his eyes and fought to get his breathing under control. *Breathing won't keep your hand from coming off.*

His eyes snapped open and, without any further hesitation, he raised the katana and brought it down upon his wrist. There was a blinding flash of excruciating pain and he almost blacked out. He avoided looking down; he desperately did not want to see the carnage.

Chloe knelt and wrapped his new stump in the cloth which became completely dyed red within moments. The simple act of her touching the bloody end of his arm blasted more pain through him.

"Well done, Falconer-san!" Yoshikazu said.

Kyle knew his face must have been contorted into a macabre grimace. He hadn't noticed how much he was sweating until this moment. His soaked shirt clung to his body as if he had gone for a swim in it.

His friends helped him over to the couch where Toshiyama still sat with his mutilated arm clutched to his chest. The giant smiled derisively at seeing Kyle in the same state as himself. *Yeah, well, I've still got one hand.*

"Jesus," Jazmine said. "How do you feel?"

He responded, "Like when I first got my vampire hunger pangs, only a hundred times worse. I might throw up on you in a sec."

Chloe, who sat next to him, offered him her hand. "Feed."

"No, Chloe, I can't do that to you again," he protested.

"She's right," Mel said. "You'll feel better once you've got more blood in you. I don't know if you noticed, but you just lost a lot only a few feet away."

Kyle still felt bad about nearly killing Chloe the first time he sucked her, and this time he was in so much worse shape. He was afraid he would bleed her dry. He sighed. "Just promise to take your arm back before I go too far."

"Promise," she said.

He shakily put his remaining hand on her palm. Her essence began flowing into him. Within moments, his nausea receded, albeit not entirely. The pain was still intense, but within a minute, it too, subsided.

Chloe took her arm back as promised and Kyle breathed a sigh of relief. He had gotten through this. Now all he had to do was stop an impending holy war. Piece of cake. "I don't know about you guys, but I'm ready to go home." Funny; he now viewed the loft as his home.

Sakazuki and Yoshikazu, who had been conferring on the other side of the room, came over. "One moment, please."

"What is it now?" Jazmine said testily.

Sakazuki explained, "Falconer-san, you have impressed us with your fortitude, ability, and commitment to honor. We have a tradition in our country. We bond by exchanging cups of sake. We ask that you join us in forging a new friendship."

Well, that was news to Kyle. He had come here as an enemy and now they wanted to be BFFs. "One of your guys just tried to kill me ten minutes ago," he reminded them.

"Yes, but in prevailing, you proved your mettle. Had you only cut off your hand, we would have sent you on your way without a second thought. But since you also survived meiyo kettou, you have wowed us, as you say. We would be honored to count you as *nakama,* an ally."

"Fine, sure, I guess," Kyle said. He felt he could once again hold down some alcohol.

"Excellent!" Sakazuki said before shouting instructions to everyone in Japanese.

They brought in another low table, only this one was long enough for five people on each side. They put it down in the center of the dance floor. Kyle sat in the middle, with Chloe and Shaun on either side of him, and Jazmine and Mel on opposite ends. In front of them sat Sakazuki, Yoshikazu, and Toshiyama who still sneered.

The attendant brought in a piece of fine Japanese pottery in roughly the shape of a health potion in RPGs. Everyone at the table was handed a tiny bowl which evidently served as a cup.

"It is customary to pour another's drink rather than your own," Yoshikazu said. With that in mind, Kyle poured Chloe and Shaun's drinks.

"*Kanpai!*" Sakazuki said. Everyone took a drink. Kyle held his cup with his remaining hand. His throat burned with the sweet-tasting mana flowing through it, but it still tasted like victory.

"You are now brothers with us," Yoshikazu said.

"Ahem," Mel said.

"And sisters," Sakazuki added.

Both Japanese men beamed excitedly. Toshiyama grunted.

"Tell us about your *kazoku,*" Yoshikazu said.

"Our what?" Kyle said.

"Ah. I apologize. I do not remember your word for a vampire family."

"Oh, a manzil?" Kyle said, shrugging. "We're not one. We're just... friends, I guess?"

Jazmine explained, "Yeah, you have to get permission from the Guide to start a manzil."

Sakazuki grunted. The oyabun then said, "Japan is independent. We do not follow those rules."

"Ah, yes. The Osaka Accord of 1820," Mel said.

"That's right," Shaun said. "Our peoples were at war for centuries. The Guide wanted to bring all vampires under their control, but they underestimated the *bushido*. Our sacred code helped us to fight them to a stalemate despite their superior numbers."

"Were you there, Shaun?" Kyle asked.

He smiled. "Nah, not me. I was turned about twenty years ago. I've spent most of my existence in America."

"Who... ungh... turned... you?" Chloe said.

"The love of my life, and I'll keep it at that for now." He was still smiling.

Sakazuki had a perplexed look on his face. "How did you five come together?" They explained it for the hundredth time to him and he sighed. "I knew there were violent vampires here in New York, but I never suspected they were planning a holy war.

"We cannot help you with this, sadly. Not directly, anyway. That many vampires fighting out in the open would bring too much attention upon our species. We can, however, assist you in other ways."

"Like what?" Kyle said.

"You'll be at a severe disadvantage facing that manzil with only one hand. We can give you a new one. A stronger one."

The offer certainly sounded good, but Kyle was a bit skeptical. "Even stronger than my vampire strength?"

"It is made of enhanced titanium. At your current level, I would say it would be 1.5 times stronger. As you gain strength, however, that may change."

"All right," Kyle said. "I'm sold. When can you put it on me?"

Yoshikazu said, "We do not have it on hand, but we can have it flown in. Give us two days."

Jazmine frowned. "That's cutting it pretty close. There are only three days until the Grand Imam arrives."

Sakazuki put up his hands in an appeasing gesture. "The operation will be quick and Falconer-san will be back on his feet within the hour. You have my word."

"Let's put it on the schedule, then. Can we get a reminder card?" Mel said sarcastically.

"Meet us again here forty-eight hours from now. We have a medical facility aboard this yacht," Sakazuki said.

"Sounds good," Kyle said.

* * *

Upon returning to the loft, Kyle and Chloe retired to the guest room. Kyle collapsed onto the bed. There was a dull ache in his new stump. He took heavy breaths.

"All... right?" Chloe lay down beside him.

He sighed. "I put on a brave front back there, but I'm hurting in more ways than one. I've been through hell repeatedly since arriving in this city."

"Talk?" she said. "Alsakina?"

He shook his head. "I don't think I can manage that right now. Any talking will have to be done like this."

"Tell... me. Pain."

He explained, "Most people don't go through anything close to what I've been through the past few weeks. I lost my friends, I lost my family, I've come so close to losing my faith. I've been brought to the edge of madness repeatedly.

"What's it all for? What does God expect me to do here? I don't have any answers. The only answer I have is you."

She raised an eyebrow. "Me?"

"Yes. I think God sent you and the others to keep me together while I carry out his mission of stopping Kyrios. I would have been completely lost without you guys. But especially you, Chloe. I need you right now."

She grinned at him. "Sweet." She then put a hand on his stump and squeezed. The pain was worth the pleasure.

16

December 11.
Chloe laced Kyle's skates as they prepared to venture onto the ice at Rockefeller Center. This had been her idea. "'I've always wanted to go, but Kyrios would never let me,'" she had read from a card earlier. Despite his disability, he happily agreed. He had never been ice-skating, either, and it sounded like fun. On the way to the rink, they had bought prepaid mobile phones.

The whole place was lit up as a multi-colored wonderland. On one side of the rink, behind the railing, loomed the famous golden statue of Prometheus, and towering even above that was the iconic Christmas tree put up every year at this location. Throngs of people cavorted on the ice; some skated shakily, trying not to topple over, while others *did* topple and fall on their butts. A proud few danced around like it was the Winter Olympics. Kyle had a pretty good idea where he would find himself on the skating spectrum. Then, again, he had displayed quite the agility while fighting Chloe atop the church. Although, that was with all four limbs.

Chloe took him by the arm and led him out onto the ice. *We must make quite the couple—an albino and a one-handed man.* He tensed up as his skates landed on the ice...

...and they immediately slipped and plummeted. Chloe ended up on top of him, her legs resting on his head while her upper body was on the ice. They laughed. *I guess preternatural agility doesn't always kick in for the undead.*

He got to one knee and she helped him to his feet. The warmth in her face when she looked at him got him excited down below. It wasn't exactly lust, but something much more meaningful.

She grabbed him firmly and they began moving forward on unsteady feet. There was an ever-present danger of making fools of themselves, but Kyle didn't care. Left foot. Right foot. Left foot. Right foot. "I was afraid all we'd have to bond over was our shared trauma. But we have this wonderful experience tonight. Thank you, Chloe."

"Welcome," She beamed from ear to ear.

The pulse of the city beat all around them. Everything and everyone felt so alive. "Concrete jungle" seemed too crude a description for the beauty and majesty of New York.

A thought occurred to him. "How long have you been in this city?"

"Whole... life. Lived in... Laurelton." He didn't know exactly where that was, and he didn't want to torture her by asking for more details.

"Wow," he said. "So, for you, this place was a prison."

"Yes. But... not... ungh... anymore. Am... free."

They hit the far wall and turned left. "That's right. I'll fight to keep you from ever being imprisoned again."

"So... sweet." She abruptly kissed him on the cheek, sending another jolt of pleasure through him. Vampires really did move quickly.

Afterward, they went to Meravigliosa Italia, an all-night Italian restaurant nearby. On the wall above their table was a beautiful fresco of Tuscany with a gorgeous sunset overlooking Florence.

When the waiter came to take their order, Kyle decided to go with traditional lasagna. Chloe, however, pulled out a card and read from it. "'I want the spaghetti with no sauce or toppings. Just plain spaghetti.'"

"You mean, just the noodles?" Kyle said.

She nodded. The waiter still complimented her choice and went away to deliver the order.

"You don't like the sauce?"

Having obviously anticipated the question, she took out another card. "'I don't like tomatoes. And the sauce reminds me of all the people I've had to kill. Besides, spaghetti is delicious enough on its own.'"

"Can't argue with that," Kyle said, preferring not to comment on her past when they were having a good time. "I don't like tomatoes, either. To be honest, I don't really know much about Italian food. There aren't any Italian places in Perry, and it's never really appealed to me much."

"Love... Italian."

"Really? Kyrios let you eat it even though there's no need?"

"Tried... to... ungh... keep..." She paused to rest her brain. "Us... happy."

"So, he would throw you a bone every now and then?" She nodded. "Well, I guess even though there's no physical benefit to eating normal food, there is still an emotional one."

"Mmm," she grunted in agreement.

"I've always been partial to Chinese food myself. I *love* sweet and sour chicken. I know a place back home that would give you a ton of it for six dollars. Of course, part of me now thinks it's kind of a waste to buy food we don't need."

"Emotional... benefit," she reminded him.

"Yeah, I've got to keep that in mind."

The waiter soon brought their meals. Chloe grabbed a fork and was about to dig in when Kyle said, "Wait. Can you indulge in something?"

She responded with a raised eyebrow but nodded.

He took her hands in his and allowed himself a moment to revel in the electricity before focusing on the task at hand and closing his eyes. "Dear Heavenly Father, we thank you for this food even though our status is less than holy. Thank you for allowing us this small comfort in these dangerous times. Please give us strength as we seek to defeat Kyrios and save the world. Amen."

"Amen." He hadn't expected Chloe to say it, so he was pleasantly surprised by this.

"I meant what I said," he said. "Someday, I'll find God and get him to forgive you." He probably could have included that in the prayer, but it was a bit too personal for a public place such as this. Besides, you couldn't ask that over the prayer phone. It had to be in person. Man-to-man. Or man-to-God.

"Good... man," she said, smiling. "My... heart... ungh... better."

✳ ✳ ✳

Finally, the time came to go meet back up with the Office on their yacht. Kyle was even more tense than usual. The Grand Imam arrived tomorrow night, and with him, the potential for an apocalypse. "I sure hope Angelica knows what she's doing," Kyle said as they drove to the pier.

"We can't count on Redeemers for this," Mel said.

"That's right," Jazmine affirmed. "She might be willing to let us be, but her *friends* won't. If they show up, it'll be that much more dangerous for us."

"And yet, don't we kind of need backup here? The Office won't get involved directly, so friends might be a good thing," Shaun said.

"*Your* friends are the reason Kyle needs a new hand," Jazmine said.

Keeping his eyes firmly on the road, Shaun said, "But if this hadn't happened, he wouldn't have gotten the key to beating Kyrios."

"We could have found another way," Mel said.

"Enough," Kyle said. "You're both right. But this is the way things turned out, so we just have to deal with it." His seat had arm rests, though his left arm fit entirely on it rather than hanging off as his right arm did. This made him feel emotionally ill in the pit of his stomach. But then again, so did most things these days.

Chloe, sitting on his right, took his hand in hers. This comforted him and helped his heart rate to go down. He found himself able to breathe normally again.

They soon arrived at the pier where they were once again taken into the *Nagareboshi*. This time they went even deeper than the dance floor and into the med bay. It consisted of a row of a dozen beds, each separated by curtains. A table with a computer on it lay at the far end, and there were shelves containing medical supplies on either side of it.

A short, balding Japanese man with a green mask and scrubs came over to greet them. *"Konnichi wa. Boku wa kono shujutsu no tame ni Farukana-san no isha desu."*

"Anyone catch that?" Mel said.

"I understood 'konnichi wa.' That means 'hello,' right?" Kyle said.

"Yes," Shaun said. "He introduced himself as your doctor for the operation."

"Oh. Uh, konnichi wa," he said, bowing.

The doctor bowed back, and Yoshikazu and Sakazuki entered. "Hello, Falconer-san! This is Dr. Kanazawa. He will be taking care of you," Yoshikazu said.

Across from the beds was a larger space where an operating table sat. They instructed Kyle to change into a hospital gown and lie down on it. His friends were escorted out of the room.

They put an anesthetic mask over him, and that was the last thing he remembered.

✳ ✳ ✳

Jazmine, Mel, Chloe, and Shaun sat on the couch on the dance floor above. "Are you going to be okay being away from your job?" Jazmine said to Mel.

"It's fine," Mel said. "It just builds anticipation for my next performance."

"What is it you do?" Shaun said. He sat on the right of them.

Mel shot him a proud smile. "I'm a lounge singer."

"That's how we met," Jazmine said. "For me, it was love at first sight."

"Was it the same for you, Mel?"

"Not exactly. I don't know what Jazmine told you, but I'm not gay in the strictest sense. I'm pansexual. I'm attracted to a person's energy."

"Whereas I'm OG gay," Jazmine said.

"That's interesting," Shaun said.

"What about you?" Mel said. "Anyone special in your life?"

"There was. A long time ago. But that's a story for another time."

"What about you, Chloe?" Jazmine said.

"Moonlight... bonding... now."

Both Jazmine and Mel went "Oooh!" at the same time.

"It's gotta be with Sour Cream," Jazmine said.

"Don't... jinx," Chloe said.

They all laughed. "You're a strange one, Chloe," Jazmine said. "White as a ghost and limited in speech."

"Not... freak," Chloe said, incensed.

"Sorry," Jazmine said. "Sometimes we don't think before we speak. Isn't that right, Cocoa?"

"Yeah..." Mel said. "Jaz doesn't mean anything by it. She likes to rib people."

Shaun raised an eyebrow. "'Cocoa'?"

Jazmine explained, "That's what I call Mel because she's dark and comforting to me."

"Don't embarrass me!" Mel said, grinning from ear to ear.

Chloe glanced over at the stairs. She hoped Kyle was all right.

* * *

Kyle opened his eyes. He was on one of the beds in the med bay. He was still groggy.

Dr. Kanazawa approached with Yoshikazu. "You're awake," the latter said.

"Ung. Yeah," Kyle replied.

"Take a look!" Yoshikazu said.

At first, Kyle didn't know what he meant. Then he remembered the operation. He brought his left arm up and laid eyes on his new hand. It was silver and sleek, each part of it perfectly proportioned to fit his body. He tried wiggling his new metal fingers and was able to do so with ease. "What's the Japanese word for 'awesome'?"

"That would be *sugoi,*" Yoshikazu said.

"Sugoi, then." He smiled and touched the metal surface with his other hand. It was cold, though not as cold as the rest of his body. There was also a scar around his wrist where flesh met metal.

"That will heal within twenty-four hours," Yoshikazu said.

He escorted Kyle back up to the dance floor. His friends rushed over to greet him. "Okay?" Chloe said.

"I'm feeling pretty good," Kyle confirmed.

"Nice hand job!" Jazmine joked. That made Kyle blush.

Shaun's eyes went wide when he saw the new hand. "You're like the bad guy in *Enter the Dragon* now!" Imitating Jim Kelly, he said, "'Man, you're like out of a comic book!'"

"That's offensive," Mel said. Nevertheless, she smiled. "I'll never forgive Bruce Lee for killing the one brother in that movie."

Toshiyama thundered over and looked at the new hand. He grunted and raised the arm that Kyle had removed the hand from two nights ago. He had the same hand. "You gave one to him?" Kyle said.

By now, Sakazuki had joined them. "A yakuza with no hands isn't useful for much. Cutting off his remaining hand wasn't originally part of his punishment. You did that on your own, Falconer-san, rather than kill him."

"I stand by my decision," Kyle said.

"You are most honorable," Sakazuki said.

Kyle's prepaid phone vibrated. He took a look at it. "I just got a text from Angelica. She sent us a bunch of info about tomorrow night."

"Good," Jazmine said. "Let's get back and come up with a game plan."

Kyle bowed to Sakazuki. "Thanks for everything, but we have to go now."

Sakazuki said, "Perhaps we can be of assistance again after this crisis is over."

"Hopefully, that won't be necessary," Kyle said. "But if it comes to that, I'll make sure to be useful to you as well."

"Farewell then, Falconer-san."

* * *

They reconvened back at the loft in the kitchen. Kyle explained the new info. "Angelica says the Grand Imam's flight will arrive at midnight tomorrow. The gate has still not been assigned and likely won't be until the last minute. However, there will be Redeemers there. Angelica requested reinforcements."

Mel said, "All right, so we infiltrate JFK with plenty of time to spare. We look for out-of-place Arabs and take them down."

"They're not all Arabs," Kyle said. "Amelie is French and Cortez is a Spaniard.

Jazmine shrugged. "Fine, we'll add Spaniards and French women to the list. Can't be many of those running around at the airport." Mel rolled her eyes affectionately.

"What will be the infiltration point?" Shaun said.

There was a map of the airport on the kitchen island. "I suggest we avoid coming in from a distance by not crossing the busy streets that run around the airport such as North Service Road, JFK Expressway, and the Van Wyck Expressway. We're at a higher risk of being spotted the longer we have to travel on foot."

"How'd you get to be such a sneak?" Jazmine said.

Kyle shrugged. "I played a lot of Metal Gear Solid and Splinter Cell as a kid."

"I totally pegged you for a nerd," Mel jested.

Shaun pumped a fist. "Hideo Kojima! I love him!"

"Back... to... ungh... business."

Kyle said, "Chloe's right. Let's stay focused. Okay, so the way I see it, the best way to infiltrate the airport is just to drive right in."

"Wait a minute!" Shaun said. "You want to risk my van in this?"

"That depends. Who is it registered to?"

Confusion showed on Shaun's face. "Uh, well, it's registered to *me*. Shaun Mifune. A lot of vampires change their registration information every few decades, but I haven't been one long enough to need to do that."

Kyle frowned. "So, if something goes wrong and the authorities find it, they can trace it back to you?"

"Yes."

Everyone was silent for a moment. Finally, Jazmine said, "What if we rented a car for this? We could give them fake information and no one would be any the wiser."

Kyle thought about it. "To rent a car, you need a valid driver's license and a credit card. Do either of you happen to have both in a different name?"

"Yeah," Mel said. "As undead monsters, we need to have multiple identities. And we don't go by our real names, anyway. 'Jazmine' and 'Mel' are aliases."

"Knew... it."

"You did not," Kyle said to Chloe.

"Did... so."

"Look, I don't care what your real names are," Kyle said. "What's important is actions, and you've convinced me I can trust you."

"Thanks, Sour Cream!"

"Besides," Kyle said, and a devious grin adorned his face. "I know where you live."

Mel smiled. "It's good to see you smiling after everything that's happened. I would've been afraid to go into battle with a broken boy."

"One day at a time," Kyle said.

They all smiled. "So, we rent a car, we drive it into the airport, we park it there, and we go off looking for Kyrios," Shaun said.

Kyle shook his head. "I think we need an extra step here."

"You want to buy plane tickets so we can get into the terminal," Jazmine said.

Kyle pointed an index finger at her. "Bingo. If we're caught in there without the marks on our boarding passes made by security as we pass through, we'll be in trouble. Any attention we draw could also alert Kyrios."

"Leave it to us," Mel said. "I'm guessing you don't have a ton of money on you."

"I work in a supermarket deli—or, at least, I used to—so, no. Up until recently, I was a poor college student. The 'poor' part still applies, even if nothing else does."

The mood became somber again. "I'm sorry, Kyle," Jazmine said, using his real name for a change. "Mel and I were turned willingly, but you're maleun."

"What's that?"

190

"I guess nobody told you about the terms for a turned person. *Saeid* are people who were turned willingly, while *maleun* were turned against their will."

"I... maleun," Chloe said.

"For me, it's a bit of both," Shaun said.

"Be careful, Kyle. There's a stigma around maleun," Mel said. "Saeid tend to look down on them. Now, me and Jaz, we're open-minded."

"Great," Kyle said before yawning. "I'd love to stay and chat, but I have had a busy night. I'm gonna hit the hay."

"Me... too." She was probably tired from getting drained earlier.

"Go ahead," Mel said. "We'll search for plane tickets. It's short notice, but I'm sure we can find *something*."

"And I will go home as well. *Ciao!*" Shaun said.

"Don't you mean *sayonara?*" Jazmine teased.

He grinned sheepishly and left.

* * *

December 13.

Angelica stood outside Gate 23B in the terminal at JFK the next morning. Normally guests weren't allowed this far into the facility, but she still had special clearance. The area was filled with the chatter of many different languages, and more types of clothing than she could take in.

The Grand Imam would arrive tonight, and despite her cool exterior, she was apprehensive about everything. If they failed, the prophecy would come true. And yet, prophecies were meant to come true, weren't they? Especially one that came from the Madonna. God was infallible, so could this even be stopped? She told herself there must be; surely, God would not allow a holy war to be carried out.

She still didn't know what to make of that quasi-manzil Kyle Falconer belonged to. They seemed harmless, but they were demonic in nature. Yet she didn't sense any malice from them. What did it mean? All Redeemers were taught all vampires must be destroyed. They defiled the body of Christ and were forsaken by the Father. They fed on innocent people and butchered countless others. They were her enemy. And yet...

The plane she awaited presently arrived and she stood patiently as everyone disembarked. Mistral Air Flight 139 had left the Vatican nine hours earlier and doubtless, all aboard were looking to rest. Most of them would have to wait until they either got home or got to their hotel.

But not the four individuals who now approached her after disembarking.

Wait.

Four?

"Where are the rest of you?" she said.

The plainclothes Redeemers before her consisted of Ariel, Nico, Francesco, and Elizabeth (who was the only non-Italian among them). "Apologies," Ariel said. Her ebony skin contrasted with the whiter hues of her compatriots. "We are all they could spare."

Angelica was fuming. "What do you mean, 'all they could spare'?"

Nico, a swarthy figure, ran a hand through his slick black hair. "The Schwarzbach manzil is causing trouble in Austria."

"Yes," Elizabeth said in her Scottish accent. Her tightly-cut blonde hair made her stand out from the others. That, and her five-foot-nine height. "They slaughtered an entire village and the citizens have put pressure on the government, and they, in turn, have put pressure on *us,* to act."

Francesco said nothing. The lanky Italian was, in fact, mute. But what he lacked in vocals, he made up for in fighting spirit.

"Damn them!" Angelica said, though not loud enough for the people around them to hear. She didn't care if it was blasphemy. "The prophecy is *this close* to coming true. We may only get one chance to stop it, and they send a meager four Redeemers to assist me."

Ariel explained, "His Holiness disagrees with your interpretation of the prophecy. He believes the odds are more in favor of the Schwarzbach manzil's mounting bloodshed being the true cause of the world's destruction."

"After all," Nico said, "We only have your instinct to go on." Angelica hadn't told them about Kyle Falconer's group giving her intel and possibly assisting in this operation. How could she? They'd recall her to the Vatican for mental examination if they knew she was taking help from vampires. They might even do worse. The Church had evolved since the days of old, but they could still be merciless when it came to unholy matters. All they knew was Falconer had been turned, but she had made it seem as if she hadn't encountered him.

But Elizabeth said, "Let's not discount the threat posed by the manzil here in New York. They've already proven their merciless ruthlessness. Even if nothing else, we can eliminate a few abominations while we're here.

"Now, then. Where can we get some rest?"

Angelica sighed. She would have to make do. She found herself eerily grateful for Kyle Falconer's help. Grateful to a vampire. What was the world coming to? "The airport is allowing us to use their crew rooms for the time being. Rest up and report back to me at five."

The newcomers made the sign of the cross and followed her to their quarters. Despite their doubts, they would obey her commands because she held the rank of Senior Purge Specialist.

17

Because it was winter, the sun went down a little after six. This gave Kyle and his friends just under six hours to get to the airport and save the Grand Imam.

They parked Shaun's van on Old South Road a few blocks north of Nassau Expressway and walked to the rental car place that lay in between. They managed to secure a nondescript beige sedan (the rental car people had tried to rent them a pricier minivan, but Jazmine and Mel were having none of it). As they drove on to the airport a short distance away, minuscule white blobs hit the windshield.

"Hey, it's snowing!" Shaun said as he drove them.

"Just great," Jazmine said. "Less visibility for us."

"Yes, but that means less visibility for our enemies," Mel said.

"Cancel... flight?" Chloe said.

"Good question. I'm starting to come around to Angelica's point of view. What if they cancel or divert the Grand Imam's flight due to weather? We'd lose our chance to stop Kyrios," Kyle said.

Mel shrugged. "We may be strong, but we can't defeat nature. Whatever happens, happens." She was right, of course. Their success tonight largely depended on forces outside their control." Kyle wondered if the snow was part of God's plan. Did God even exist, or was everything controlled by nature and man? He had been going back and forth on this ever since being turned.

His friends' butchered bodies.

He knew one thing for sure: *Kyrios'* plan had no place in this world.

When they got to the airport proper, they made sure to park in the nearest spot to the exit they could find to assist with a speedy escape when this was over.

"All right, let's get a move on," Mel said.

"What airline are we 'flying'?" Shaun said.

Jazmine handed them their boarding passes which she had printed off earlier. "We're flying Logic Air. It's, well, it's a cheapo airline. I figured it doesn't matter since we're not actually boarding anything."

They made their way to Terminal 8 on the airport's northwest side. Inside was a baggage claim area. A crowd was gathered around a photogenic newswoman and her cameraman. She appeared to be speaking to her anchor back at the studio. The five of them walked over to check it out and see if they could spot any members of the Kyrios manzil skulking about.

"Rich, I'm here at John F. Kennedy International Airport where a mob of people has come to greet the Grand Imam when he arrives in a little under five hours. Security is tight here, and both local and airport police have their hands full. I've had a chance to watch the trepidation in their eyes as they do their best to prevent a war from breaking out here tonight. As you know, the leader of radical group Ealim al'Ahlam, Yousef Al-Bakir, has vowed to carry out a holy war if any harm comes to our visitor tonight. Judging by their actions in London last week, it seems clear they mean what they say. The radical *Christian* group David's Purge has promised to kill the religious leader if he touches down here at JFK."

Kyle looked over at Chloe whose shoulders slumped. She had to live with her involvement with David's Purge for the rest of her life.

They studied the throng of people around the newswoman. Most of the remaining members of the Kyrios manzil were Middle Eastern, but that didn't help here. Most of the people in the terminal were Middle Eastern, some holding anti-American signs that read "Down with the Imperialists!" "Great Satan Be Gone!" and "Purify Our Sacred Land."

Kyle leaned in to whisper to Chloe. "See any of them?" She shook her head. "Okay, let's continue on."

They proceeded to go through airport security without incident. Well, aside from Kyle's new hand getting thoroughly scrutinized. Jazmine and Mel traded good-natured barbs with the black members of the security team. Once they were in the larger part of the terminal, the airport opened up. Flags from every nation hung from the ceiling and firmly cemented the international atmosphere. Shops and kiosks abounded, and the more energy-starved travelers could ride the walkway which went down the hallway.

"Okay," Kyle said. "We've all got our phones. Let's split up and look for anyone suspicious."

An hour later, Kyle sat down in a chair in one of the gates in Terminal 4. He had gone clockwise around the north end of the airport. He decided to stop in this terminal because this was the international terminal and he figured the Grand Imam would arrive here. However, he didn't know for sure, so he had sent the others in different directions.

His phone buzzed. There was a text from Angelica. It read, "C34." Kyle smiled anxiously and forwarded the message to the others. They now knew the gate their VIP would arrive at.

They soon made their way over to him. "Now we know the gate, but what's the plan? We still don't know how Kyrios will attack. Will he wait until the Grand Imam is in the building, or will he attack the plane as it's landing? Hell, he could have a surface-to-air missile for all we know," Mel said.

Kyle shrugged. "There's nothing we can do about it if he does. We'll just have to rely on the *official* security to stop any threats from the air."

"Why don't we split up again?" Shaun said. Some of us wait near the runway, while the others wait inside."

"Good idea," Kyle said. "How about Jazmine and Mel stay inside, while the rest of us go outside?"

"Oh, sure, keep the sisters inside," Jazmine teased.

"It doesn't matter to me," Kyle said.

"Fine, fine; we'll stay in here," Mel said.

"All right," Kyle said. Me, Chloe, and Shaun will go outside, activate Thief in the Night, and make our way to the runway. We'll wait there until the plane arrives."

"Don't get flattened by said plane, Sour Cream." Jazmine laughed.

Kyle grinned. "Yeah, it's gonna be real hard to hear that thing coming down on us."

Chloe snickered.

* * *

Kyle, Chloe, and Shaun passed the "No-reentry" signs that signaled the airport exits. They stepped outside into the cold December air. The snow was still coming down lightly but was nothing they thought would stop the Grand Imam's flight. Their breaths came out in visible bursts of warm air.

"I hope we made the right decision," Shaun said. "We won't be able to get back in if there's trouble at the gate."

"We have no choice but to take risks since we don't know exactly what the manzil will do.

"Come on. Let's find a secluded area to cloak ourselves in."

* * *

Nico waited on the terminal roof with his high-powered sniper rifle looking down at the runway the Grand Imam's flight would come in on. Pretty soon the FAA would halt all traffic coming in and out of the airport to secure the airspace. Any suspicious aircraft that violated it and refused to identify themselves would be shot down. Therefore, the Redeemers weren't worried about an attack from another plane.

His compatriots were stationed around the other buildings in case of an attack. Their enhanced senses would allow them to spot trouble faster than a normal human. Too bad they didn't have resistance to cold because it was bone-chilling tonight. His thermal suit helped mitigate it, but not completely. He wanted to be done with this so he could try New York's famous pizza and see how it compared to that of Italy. The Americans took pride in their pizza, but so did he.

Something below caught his attention. An amorphous blob of darkness ambled towards the runway. It was darker than the area around it, a possible indication Thief in the Night was being utilized.

He activated the comm unit in his ear. "Damascus to the Holy Land. I'm seeing a possible vampire intrusion. Could be nothing, but someone should check it out."

"This is Bethlehem. Where are you seeing it?" Ariel said.

He replied, "South of the runway and slightly west of the terminal."

"This is Jerusalem. I'll take a look," Angelica said.

"Be careful," Nico said.

"Hmph. No vampires are taking *me* unawares."

✻ ✻ ✻

Angelica crept over to where Nico said the possible vampires were. Sure enough, someone was using Thief in the Night. Her infrared goggles showed her a much darker spot than everything around it.

She intentionally shut off her comm unit. If these vampires were friendly (what a strange thought!), she didn't want to expose them—and herself for aiding them. Then again, if they were hostile, they might get the drop on her. She decided to take the risk.

The dark spot was on the wall of the terminal itself. She went over to it and said, "Identify yourself." Her crossbow was leveled and prepared for a confrontation.

"It's us," came the voice of Kyle Falconer. "Here, we'll show you."

"Don't," she said. "My allies will see you. What is your plan?"

The darkness said, "Mel and Jazmine are inside in case Kyrios attacks in there. We're out here to fight off an outside attack."

Angelica lowered her weapon while being careful to keep her back (and lips) to the other Redeemers. Her body language indicated she hadn't seen anything out of the ordinary. Her head looked around to give the impression she hadn't found anything.

"It won't do them any good to be inside. The Grand Imam isn't going to enter the terminal like a normal passenger. He will disembark on the runway and be taken by car to a VIP suite elsewhere at the airport."

"Thanks," Kyle said. "We'll get them down here, then."

She warned him, "Don't show yourselves if at all possible. My team will blow your heads off if they spot you."

"Good to know." He sounded nervous, as well he should be.

She left the area and reactivated her comm unit. "It was nothing. There were no vampires."

"I could have sworn I saw it!" Nico said.

"You're still relatively new. In time, you'll get better at differentiating between natural darkness and the undead," Elizabeth said.

"You just want to blow them away and get that pizza," Francesco joked.

"They say it's super good!"

"Enough chatter," Angelica said. "Keep quiet unless you have something important to say. Jerusalem out."

It was only a few minutes until the Grand Imam's flight would arrive. The five friends stood cloaked in darkness against the wall of the terminal and stared at the runway. By this point, the area around the gate had filled up with police cars and other emergency vehicles off to the side. Kyle had never kept Thief in the Night going for this long, and he hoped there wasn't a limit to it.

The planes had long since been grounded, but the stillness was broken by the roar of a jet engine. "Someone's coming to visit," Jazmine said. It was meant to be a joke, but none of them were in a jovial mood. There was a heaviness in Kyle's stomach, the kind he used to get when he got called to the principal's office. But the lesson being taught at this school was religious cleansing by a madman.

Chloe pointed to the sky. "There."

"Yeah, that must be it," Kyle said.

A faint blur of lights in the distant sky heralded the arrival of the Grand Imam. As it got closer, they could see it was a massive plane on par with Air Force One, albeit with gold Egyptian writing on the side. This guy knew how to travel.

It soon hit the ground and roared down the runway, blasting exhaust, to an eventual stop. A few minutes passed, and it began taxiing towards them. Kyle was breathing heavily now and he was scared. With each moment that passed, the threat of mass genocide became increasingly real.

The plane stopped about a hundred yards from the gate and the engine was shut off. The police and other black security vehicles rushed over to protect the disembarking dignitary. They assumed positions around the plane like a wagon train in the old movies his dad liked. A limo then came over and parked near the exit ramp.

* * *

The Grand Imam Abdul Batin Rabbani emerged from the cabin flanked by his security team. He resembled a typical Middle Eastern religious leader with his graying beard, white *kufi* hat, and black *abaya* shirt with matching dress pants. He did not indulge in Western excesses such as drugs and alcohol which resulted in his slim figure.

He descended the steps, every eye around him alert for trouble. He was tired from his trip and wanted to rest.

The limo at the bottom opened up and a familiar face emerged. "Hey, buddy! Welcome to America. You're gonna love it here. It's fantastic!"

Rabbani sighed. "President Jericho. Thank you for meeting me here. And you can drop the act."

When he hit the ground, William Jericho struck out with his meaty palm for a handshake. "Number one rule of leadership: Always make your enemies underestimate you."

"Yes, I'm sure your enemies do not think highly of you."

Jericho beamed. "That's the idea. Now, come on; let's tie one on." A sudden wind kicked up, and he had to hold down his toupee.

"I would like to get to my suite now if you don't mind," Rabbani said.

"Fine, spoilsport." Men like Jericho were the reason Rabbani hated this country. They enabled the constant deluge of murders that occurred seemingly around the clock by deflecting responsibility to protect their people. That, and they drank to excess. Alcohol was *haram*, or prohibited, to most Muslims.

One of Jericho's Secret Service agents put a finger against his earpiece and cocked his head, listening to something. He then grabbed Jericho. "Mr. President, we have to go. *Now.* There's a situation."

"Shit," Jericho said. "You guys better deal with it."

"We will, sir. But you and the Grand Imam need to get in the car." Jericho's motorcade vehicle was, of course, bulletproof."

The screaming of tires in the distance told them this was real.

* * *

"What the hell is that?" Jazmine said.

They looked to where she was pointing. A pair of hulking vehicles sped towards the Grand Imam's plane from the other side of the airport. They crashed through a security fence like it wasn't even there. The shriek of twisting metal reached their ears.

"Those are SWAT personnel carriers!" Shaun said.

"I have a feeling they're not here to protect our VIP," Kyle said. This reminded him of something. It came back to him then. The news cast at Mel's. *Police are still puzzled over the theft of two armored personnel carriers last week.*

"This is how the son of a bitch is attacking!" Mel said.

"Everybody! Run to the plane! We have to protect the Grand Imam!" Kyle said.

They disengaged Thief in the Night and rushed toward the imminent warzone.

18

Everyone in the assembled Grand Imam/Jericho group watched in horror as the behemoth vehicles came speeding at them like giant, 27,200-pound bullets. All the security personnel raised their guns and began firing at them, but Rabbani knew enough about such vehicles to realize it was futile. They might as well attack Allah with flyswatters.

One of Jericho's men yelled something at him, but nothing could be heard except for the deafening rapport of gunfire. The man pointed to the open door of Jericho's motorcade car. Rabbani wasted no time getting in. The roar of the gunfire lessened in the sealed vehicle, but it was still hard to hear anything else.

"Get us the fuck out of here!" Jericho yelled to the driver.

Rabbani looked out the window in time to see the APCs slam into the police cars, swatting them aside like cardboard in a hurricane. Now, there was nothing between them and certain death.

Rabbani was hammered by a jarring impact as an APC collided with the side of the president's car. The last thing he remembered was a blinding pain in his leg.

"Jesus Christ!" Jazmine yelled as they ran toward the carnage. The combined security team continued to unload upon the APCs. Within moments, however, the doors opened, and impossibly quick figures leapt out. They began tearing apart the defenders who couldn't land a shot because of the vampires' speed.

One of the vampires noticed them coming and waved his arm. A wall of fire shot up from the ground and surrounded the Grand Imam/Jericho group.

"Sterco!" Nico shouted. He was having a hard time getting a shot off with all the chaos swirling down there.

"Take them out!" Angelica screamed in his ear. *Easy for you to say.*

He slowed his breath to sharpen his senses. *There!* A vampire was creating a wall of flame around the vehicles. The fire obscured his vision, but he remembered where the vampire's head was. Nico squeezed the trigger.

The flames went out and the vampire who had created them dropped to the ground without his head. That left eight of them to deal with. Kyle didn't know who had fired, but he was grateful.

They leapt into the fray. Kyle began grappling with one of the Arab manzil members. This man had maniacal eyes and he threw Kyle over one of the outer police cars before standing over him in a bestial state.

* * *

Nico didn't know what on Earth was going on. "Vampires are fighting other vampires! Should I take them all out?"

"Negative," came Angelica's voice. "Right now, focus solely on the ones that came out of the APCs."

He protested, "But they're all enemies of God. Shouldn't we wipe them all out?"

"We need our priorities. We can use the enemies of the ones trying to assassinate the Grand Imam to our advantage."

"Understood." Her plan was then to keep the unknown vampires alive until they eliminated the ones threatening Rabbani. Then the area would be purged of all undead. At least, that was how he interpreted it.

One of the anti-kill-the-Grand-Imam group was on the ground and a nasty-looking vampire stood over him.

It was the easiest shot Nico ever took.

* * *

The Arab standing over Kyle lost his head just the same as his ally. Kyle got up to get back into the fight—and behind cover, in case the mystery sniper decided to target him next.

Ahead of him, most of the security detail had been massacred. Kyle spotted Kyrios ripping the passenger door off the presidential motorcade car and casually hurling it to the ground at Kyle's feet. Kyrios reached in and grabbed the unconscious form of the Grand Imam. A sense of crushing dread came over Kyle as he believed this was the moment everything would be decided.

Kyle pounded the ground with his feet and pumped his legs to get to the Grand Imam before Kyrios finished him off.

But one of the Arabs got between him and Kyrios. Kyle put up a fight, but he was too distracted by the knowledge he might already have been too late. Frustration go the better of him and, with one swift movement, he picked up the car door and swung it like a sword, decapitating the Arab with the sharp edge. *You guys are losing your heads tonight.*

Morbidly satisfied by this, he turned his attention back to Kyrios. But Kyrios was gone, and so was the Grand Imam.

Panic set in. Where did they go? Could the Grand Imam already be dead?

Without warning, one of the APCs pulled out and began speeding away from the scene. Within moments, it became cloaked in darkness. Kyle didn't know Thief in the Night could affect cars.

The others ran over to him. "He put the Grand Imam in the APC," Jazmine said.

"We have to go after them!" Mel added.

By now, more police and emergency vehicles were flooding into the area. Kyle noticed one of the police cars hadn't been hit by the APCs. He pointed to it. "Shaun! Drive!"

They scrambled to get into the car and the more experienced vampires (i.e., everyone but Kyle) cloaked the vehicle in darkness. They peeled out after the APC which they could still see through the black cloud it was enveloped in.

"They shouldn't be able to chase us now," Shaun said. "Man, this reminds me of that scene in The Dark Knight where they're chasing the Joker through the tunnel."

"Kyrios had the Grand Imam knocked out and in his hands. Why didn't he kill him?" Kyle said.

"Grand... display," Chloe said.

Kyle now understood completely. "He wants to put the exclamation point on this by televising the Grand Imam's execution. He won't kill him until they get in position. But where are they going?"

"We just have to follow them and find out," Mel said.

"Cocoa's right. Also, we should hang back for now. Any aggressive moves on our part might cause them to abandon the plan and kill the Grand Imam on the spot," Jazmine said.

"I love it when you call me Cocoa," Mel swooned. Kyle appreciated the levity during this nightmarish situation.

"Shaun, keep us at a safe distance," Kyle said. The car veered sharply to the left, narrowly avoiding an incoming vehicle at an intersection. "What the hell?"

"People can't see us," Shaun said. "That means I have to be wayyyy more careful than usual. Sorry, but I need to focus. I'm keeping a safe distance, though."

Up ahead, Kyrios wasn't displaying the same consideration. They watched as he rammed another car that had inadvertently wandered into his path. Kyle languished with the knowledge there was no time to stop and help them.

"What direction are we going?" Kyle asked.

"We're heading northeast up Springfield Boulevard, Sour Cream. We're in Cambrian Heights, now."

They were speeding through neighborhoods. This worried Kyle even more than if they had been going down a busy street. There weren't as many lights out here and they were pretty much impossible to spot to anyone who might be out and about. No matter who they might run over, they couldn't stop to help.

The APC turned right onto Jamaica Avenue, so they followed suit. Kyrios' group then got onto the Cross Island Parkway and proceeded northwest. After going that way for a bit, they turned west on Northern Boulevard, got off on Bayview Avenue, and took that for several miles until it became Westshore Boulevard, and then continued to Kings Point Road.

Eventually, the APC ran out of road at the very end of Hewlett Point. Beyond that was Long Island Sound.

"Where the hell are they going?" Jazmine said, not for the first time.

The APC went out of sight behind a house amidst the thickly-wooded area. Kyle had them stop the police car at the house so they could attempt to creep up on Kyrios and hopefully rescue the Grand Imam before the manzil leader's demonic plan could be accomplished.

However, by the time they arrived at the shore, they saw Kyrios remained a step ahead of them. The remaining manzil members hightailed it northwest away from them on speed boats.

"Where are they going?" Kyle said, sounding like a broken record.

"I don't know," Mel said. "There's nothing along their route except Hart Island." She paused for a moment. "Jesus."

"What is it?" Kyle said.

"Hart Island's a giant cemetery and nobody lives there. It's the perfect base for a psycho like Kyrios," Jazmine said.

Then that was where the final act of his unholy play would take place. "We have to get there," Kyle said.

Shaun said, "I don't see any other boats, so we'll have to use Intentional Blasphemy."

"What is that?" Kyle said.

Jazmine explained, "It's walking on the water like Jesus. The nun who comes up with these names has a sense of humor."

Kyle hadn't heard about that Satanic Feat. "How do you do it?"

"You take Thief in the Night, but you consolidate all your darkness in your feet, making it basically a black cloud you can walk on. Or run on. We're going to need to run to catch up with them."

Great. He needed to learn a new skill within minutes. Ursula had told him he was a quick learner, but the pressure was firmly on now.

He activated Thief in the Night. "Good, Sour Cream," Jazmine said. "Now, reach out and take hold of the darkness and throw it to your feet. With both hands."

Kyle reached out but his hands met only air. "It's not working. How do you grab darkness?"

"You're not thinking of the darkness as a part of you," Shaun said. "You have to treat it as a piece of your body."

Kyle closed his eyes and imagined all the space around him as his own body. He then closed his hands on something. "It's squishy," he said.

Mel said, "That's it. Now, throw it under your feet."

Kyle did so, and he sprang up a few inches. "Whoa!"

"You... did... it!"

Despite everything that was going on, he couldn't help but giggle a little. "It's like a bounce house! And this will keep me above water?"

"Damn straight, Sour Cream."

The rest of them did the same and charged out onto the water. Kyle went after them and found it less difficult than he had thought to maintain his balance on the water. The liquid seemed to stick to the darkness and not waver under it.

Mocking Jesus, though. He continued adding sins to his ledger. If he ever did meet up with God, how did he know he wouldn't be cast to Hell instantly?

They ran swiftly across Long Island Sound. The salty sea air greeted Kyle's lips. The lights of the Bronx softly lit up the western shore miles away. As for Hart Island, Kyle could make out its outline in the darkness.

They reached its shores within ten minutes. The boats greeted them, but the manzil had already departed. The island itself was partly forested but also had large acres of flat land. They had arrived at the southern tip which was a wooded area.

"Let's keep going," Kyle said.

They made their way through the trees and emerged into a flat rectangular area. There was a large complex of buildings to the north. "That building has lights on," Jazmine said. In fact, every window on the second floor was lit.

"There's not supposed to be electricity on the island. Clearly, someone's made some improvements," Mel added.

"That's our target, then," Kyle said.

There was a paved road that led right up to the building, so they rushed along it until they reached their destination. They were then able to make it out clearly. It was a U-shaped red brick building with another square brick building in front of it. Running parallel to it was a large ditch filled with rectangular crates. "What's that?" said.

"A burial plot," Mel said. "Those are coffins in there. Clearly, they're in the process of covering it back up." Indeed, there was a sizable mound of dirt nearby.

They went around the ditch and arrived in front of the U-shaped building. "The only lights are coming from upstairs," Shaun said.

They crept inside. The ground level was completely dilapidated. All sorts of detritus and dust lay on the floor, while the wallpaper hung loosely off the walls. A musky odor hit Kyle's nose. It was the smell of rot. Slim metal pillars of different colors rose from the floor to the ceiling and evidently acted as structural support. In addition, metal husks of beds lined the floor in front of the windows. This seemed to have been some sort of dormitory.

"Okay, so this place has a south side and a north side. We should split up to take both of them," Jazmine said.

It made sense to Kyle. "Chloe and I will take the north side. You three take the south side."

"Roger that, Sour Cream."

"Okay, then," Kyle said. "Come on, Chloe."

The two of them made their way across the run-down building's first floor. They soon came to a ninety-degree turn which took them west. It was going to be the same for Jazmine, Mel, and Shaun on the other side.

Eventually, they spotted a stairwell. It creaked loudly when they stepped on it, causing Kyle to almost jump out of his clothes. There was nothing they could do about it except continue up.

They emerged in light at the top of the stairs. A hall identical to the one below stretched out before them. Generators had been set up and were powering mobile lamps.

They didn't have time to think about any of that, however, as a figure in a red cloak blocked their path about ten yards away. "You two will go no further."

She pulled back her hood to reveal a lovely face. "Amelie," Chloe said.

"Kyrios is just beyond here, but you won't reach him, because I'm going to stop you here," Amelie said. Kyle was tense, but if it was only Amelie standing in their way, they had the numbers advantage even if they didn't know what her Satanic Gift was. "You're thinking you have the numbers advantage even if you don't know my Satanic Gift. But I know Chloe's, and you don't even have one yet."

An educated guess, Kyle thought. It wasn't hard to decipher what he might be thinking in this situation.

"Chloe, let her have it," he said.

Chloe summoned a handful of lightning knives and hurled them at Amelie. However, the French woman effortlessly dodged them with the grace of a psychopathic ballerina.

But that was only part of his plan. While Amelie was dodging Chloe's attack, he charged in to attack himself. He closed the distance within moments launched a series of strikes.

None of which landed. Amelie smoothly dodged that as well. Kyle decided to go for a kick next.

"You're going for a kick next," Amelie said.

He stopped short. Guessing he thought they had the numbers advantage was one thing, but how did she know he would try for a kick next?

She didn't let him ponder that for long, because she launched her hand and delivered a palm strike to his chest. It felt like he had been hit by a train and he went sailing back towards Chloe. His head slammed against the floor when he landed, causing an explosion of stars.

"Kyle!" Chloe said and knelt beside him.

"I'll be fine," he said, though he wasn't entirely confident in that. More importantly, what was up with Amelie. Could she read his mind?

"You're wondering what is up with me. Can I truly read your mind? Yes, Kyle. I can. That is my Satanic Gift. I'm telepathic." Swell. "You say that's swell, but I suspect you're being sarcastic." This was a huge problem. How could they fight her if she knew every move they would make? "You can't, Kyle."

He got to his feet still a little shaky. "Why are you doing this?"

"Why?" she said. "To eliminate every Christian from this world. Monsters like them buried me alive during the Second Crusade! I didn't do anything wrong!" She was shouting now. "Do you know what it's like to be covered with pounds and pounds of dirt and left to die?" She still had serious trauma left over from her ordeal.

Kyle smiled. He now had a plan that took advantage of her ability to read minds.

"No!" Amelie screamed. "Don't!"

"Chloe! Imagine her being buried alive. Be as detailed as possible."

"Understood," Chloe said.

He closed his eyes and pictured the French woman being thrown into a ditch before having dirt slowly shoveled onto her bound body.

"Stop!" she shrieked. Her hands clutched her head and her eyes were screwed shut.

Kyle nodded to Chloe who produced a pair of electric knives and hurled them at the horribly distracted Amelie. They exploded upon her torso, charring it black. Amelie's eyes shot open in shock before she collapsed to the ground.

"Come on!" Kyle said and they ran past her fallen form.

They didn't get far, however. An iron grip on Kyle's leg caused him to trip. "Where do you think you're going?" Amelie said, her upper body smoldering but still intact. Hate blazed in her eyes. "How dare you torture me with that thought!"

He got to her feet before Kyle did, grabbed him by the shoulders, and ran him back over to the window which looked out onto the night. She gave him a hard shove and sent his head and shoulders crashing through the glass. More stars flashed through his head, the back of which was now wet with blood. Fresh snowflakes landed on his face.

"Kyle!" Chloe said.

The vague sounds of a struggle echoed somewhere in front of him, and it took him a moment for his vision to return to normal. Amelie handily countered Chloe's attacks and delivered a strike to her heart which sent her sprawling.

"Chloe," he said, his voice weak.

He tried pushing off of the window but Amelie was back on him in an instant. She put her hands around his neck and applied inhuman pressure. "You will pay for what you did to me!"

He couldn't breathe. Amelie, despite being a woman, had as much raw strength as anyone else he had encountered over the past two weeks. Worse, hate and rage made her even stronger. Spittle now flung from her mouth as she screamed at him.

He spared a glance at Chloe. She struggled along the ground to get over to him, but she wouldn't make it in time. That meant Kyle had to get himself out of this mess. With the edges of his vision growing black, he had to act.

He had been trying to pry her arms off his windpipe, but he realized he would have to ignore instinct. He wrapped his arms around Amelie's waist as if hugging her. He then channeled the same drive he had used to break free of Angelica's bolt and shoved off the window. He picked Amelie up, turned around, and pushed her into the window sill with enough force to make her break her death grip on his neck.

With her stunned, Kyle put his artificial hand over her face and shoved her head down onto a thick shard of glass at the bottom of the window. She was impaled instantly, the shard emerging between her eyes. She continued to stare at him with enraged eyes. She babbled incoherently, her fractured brain struggling to function.

"Stand... aside," Chloe said. She had returned to her feet. She produced a lightning knife and hurled it into Amelie's chest.

The mind-reader went down for good.

They stood over her body. "How?" Chloe asked him.

"You mean, how did I do that without her knowing what I was planning? Simple. I was winging it. I didn't have a plan she could read."

"Smart."

19

Jazmine, Mel, and Shaun emerged at the top of the stairs to find three manzil members waiting for them in their signature robes. "Took you pisswipes long enough!" the one in the middle declared. By his accent, he must have been the Spaniard Cortez.

"Can I assume your friends are waiting for *our* friends at the other end of the building?" Jazmine said.

He flipped his hood back. "I don't have to tell you shit. You're all going to die along with every other Christian in this world."

"Just try it," Mel challenged.

"I'll do more than that!"

He held out his arms and a dozen swords of all different types poofed into existence above him. He then pointed at the trio and the swords flew at them at demonic speed.

Shaun leapt in front of the lovers and the swords sank deep into his flesh, exploding out of his back. "Shaun!" they yelled.

"Dumbass!" Cortez said spitefully.

But Shaun said, "I'm not as dumb as you think." He turned around to show Jazmine and Mel the hilts which protruded from his flesh. To their astonishment, the swords retreated into his body. "My Satanic Gift is the ability to absorb physical attacks as if they were blood. Comes in handy a lot." He smiled.

"That's annoying," Cortez said. "But, thankfully, I have someone who can deal with it."

More swords poofed into existence and he hurled them again.

"It's pointless!" Shaun said.

However, he saw too late the blades were not aimed at him but at the floor around his feet. They slammed into the decaying surface and punched straight through. Shaun found himself plummeting to the floor below. He landed with a hard thud. He coughed on the dust that was kicked up by this.

Cortez turned to the man to his left, one of the Arabs. "Ahmad, deal with him."

Ahmad shrugged and walked behind him a few yards before slamming his foot on the flooring and smashing it. Ahmad, too, went through it to the bottom floor.

Jazmine and Mel were now left with Cortez and the other Arab. Cortez hurled more swords at them, but they stopped abruptly in front of the women. Mel smiled. "*My* Satanic Gift is telekinesis. She pushed her arm towards their enemies and the swords flew back at them. Cortez and his comrade had to jerk aside to avoid them. The Arab muttered some curse in his native tongue.

"That's also annoying," Cortez said. "But, again, I have someone who can deal with it. Faysal, you know what to do."

The Arab began charging toward them, shaking the ground. This was surprising for someone of average height and built. Mel focused on him with her telekinesis, but to her surprise discovered she couldn't stop him. He kept on coming and closed the distance before either she or Jazmine could react. He collided with them like a quarterback and sent them hurling back to the stairs.

Jazmine groaned from atop Mel. "You all right?" With her larger size, Mel wasn't as agile as her, and she feared her partner might be at a disadvantage here.

"Yeah," Mel said. "Swell. Unh."

They got back up to see Cortez smirking up the joint. "Faysal's Satanic Feat is enhanced mass. He's far bulkier and stronger than he appears."

Jazmine said, "This is tough. Looks like it's time for the other Soul Sister to join in."

"Heh," Mel said. "Wouldn't be the same without you. By the way— 'Soul Sisters'? Was that our thing?"

"It is now."

"Alright, then."

Cortez said, "Faysal! Crush them against the wall this time and don't stop until their bones are powder."

Faysal crouched and began running at them again. Mel pushed back with her telekinesis, but this time...

Jazmine put out her hands and a hurricane-force wind began buffeting Faysal. This time, he did stop.

Cortez was feeling the effects as far back as he was. "What the hell is this?"

Jazmine explained, "Our Satanic Gifts complement each other. Together, we can push back much harder."

Both women strained against Faysal's incredible mass. Jazmine's arms felt like they would break at any moment. "Come on, Cocoa! One... more... push!"

They roared with everything they had, and finally, Faysal was sent flying backward into Cortez. The two manzil members soared across that wing of the building in a literal wind tunnel before crashing through the wall at the other end. They emerged into the black of night and disappeared.

"Elvis has left the building!" Jazmine said.

Mel laughed. "You are insane. And that's why I love you."

They embraced right there.

* * *

Shaun ran around the room trying to breathe. Ahmad was exhaling green poisonous mist which Shaun couldn't absorb. It was also affecting his vision. He coughed profusely and began staggering about.

"Now you are finished," Ahmad said. In response, Shaun renewed his efforts to get out of there, but by this point, he was disoriented and ran into a wall. He fell to his knees. *This gas is deadly even to vampires. Is this it for me? But there are so many more movies I want to watch!*

Ironically, it was his desire to consume even more pop culture that drove him to persevere. He groped around the floor for something he could use as a weapon. His lungs were about at their limit, though. He had a few more moments at most.

He cut his hand on something long and sharp. Realizing it was one of Cortez's swords, he found the hilt and picked it up.

"Just give up," Ahmad said.

Shaun wasn't sure, but he thought he could tell the location of the voice. With his time just about up, he hurled the sword in that direction.

There was a cry of pain and surprise before the mist disappeared. Ahmad collapsed onto his back, the sword having penetrated his heart.

There was a crash above him and what sounded like an explosion on the other side of the building. "Elvis has left the building!" Jazmine said.

Shaun couldn't help but laugh.

* * *

Kyle and Chloe searched rooms until they heard someone begging for his life in one. They went inside what looked like yet another dorm room, only this one was decidedly not set up like one. There was a super-expensive camcorder in front of the door which pointed at a squirming figure in a chair at the back of the room. It was the Grand Imam, and Kyrios stood behind him holding a knife.

"Kyrios!" Kyle said.

"Ah. You have arrived. You are just in time."

"You're damn right I am! You're not doing this!"

Kyrios dismissed him with a wave of his hand. "You cannot harm me, remember? So just stand there and watch the birth of a new world." He turned his attention back to the Grand Imam and spoke to the camcorder. "We are David's Purge, and tonight we are eliminating the greatest heathen alive. I am a recent convert to Christianity, but I firmly believe in our cause."

This was a live stream, and the camera was already rolling. He had two choices. He could appeal to the people watching and denounce Kyrios, but that might spur the madman into rushing to complete his horrifying mission. The other option was to attack Kyrios while he thought Kyle was still restrained by his Satanic Gift.

Kyle chose the latter and rushed Kyrios who was bringing the knife to Rabbani's throat. Kyrios noticed this but paid it no mind, clearly still confident Kyle couldn't attack him. But he was wrong. Kyle tackled him and they both crashed through the back wall and into the other room.

Kyle landed on top of Kyrios and began raining punches down on him with his metal hand. Kyrios wasn't stunned for long, however; he regained his senses and shoved Kyle off him. They got to their feet at the same time.

"How did you do that?" Kyrios said. His eyes then fell on Kyle's artificial hand. "I see. You were indeed willing to cut off a part of your own body. You have surpassed my expectations. But why oppose me? I've shown you God is not your ally or benevolent father. He has allowed all of this, even going so far as to declare my victory with the Fatima prophecy."

"I think..." Kyle said. "I think that was a warning instead of a promise. I think God sent me here to stop you."

Kyrios shook his head. "So, you believe God saves some people but not others? God plays favorites? What kind of a loving creator is that?"

"I..." He had a point. Kyle was now conflicted again. At least, about the nature of God. "I don't know about God," he admitted. "But I do know you have to be stopped regardless of religious beliefs."

Kyrios sighed. "Then I take back what I said about you surpassing my expectations. You are, in fact, a terrible disappointment. I regret wasting my time on you."

"Too bad, because this is how it is."

In his best imitation of Ursula, Kyle pivoted to deliver a graceful kick to Kyrios. But Kyrios blocked it and thrust two fingers into Kyle's throat. Kyle could have sworn his larynx was crushed at that point as he couldn't breathe and staggered, trying to avoid panicking. "You can't overcome the distance between us, Kyle. My fighting knowledge exceeds yours by many lifetimes.

Kyle's throat healed then and he could now try again. Kyrios wasn't waiting around for that to happen, though. He bent his fingers in on themselves, forming his hand into claws. He launched a strike at Kyle's chest—a typical alraqsa tactic. Kyle got an arm up and managed to deflect it, but of course, Kyrios was just getting started.

Kyrios came in with his other claw-like hand for another strike. Kyle got his knee up to block it. This wasn't a move Ursula had taught him, but she *had* said to find what worked for him.

Kyle pivoted around Kyrios and delivered a double palm strike to his back. The madman grunted loudly but held his ground. These attacks were most effective in front of the heart, but Kyle decided it would be wise to mix things up.

Kyle leveled a kick at the back of Kyrios' leg, but the manzil leader performed a standing leap into the air, contorting his body gracefully to flip over Kyle's head and land perfectly behind him. This time, he managed to deliver a successful alraqsa strike to Kyle's chest. Kyle had never had a heart attack, but he imagined it felt a lot like this. His heart seized up and he staggered back, momentarily paralyzed.

"Give up," Kyrios said. "It should be obvious by now that God has not given you the strength to beat me. Do you know why? Because he doesn't care. Not about me, and not about you. This world is nothing more than a playground full of children all the adults have abandoned. He created us and then he got bored and turned his attention elsewhere. Perhaps he created a new universe somewhere and will soon move on from that as well."

Kyle's chest ached and he succeeded in drawing in breath maybe one out of three times, but he tried not to let it show. "Yeah, God sometimes lets evil run rampant, but never forever. The Bible makes it pretty clear everyone will get their rewards and punishments in the end."

Kyrios laughed. It was a harsh and bitter sound, tinged with malice. "Is that what you obey him for, Kyle? Your reward?"

"Maybe I did once," Kyle conceded. "I was only concerned about living a holy life. But all this has taught me life is far more complicated. We can choose to live for other things. *You* can choose to live for other things."

Kyrios shook his head. "You still don't understand. I'm not looking for life. I'm looking for *death*. Many, many deaths.

"Now, then. Get out of my way or die. Either way, I'll be executing the Grand Imam within moments."

Kyle had sufficiently recovered enough to go on the attack again. That was partly the reason he had indulged Kyrios in conversation.

Kyle fainted going left but instead went right and hurled a jab at Kyrios' head. Kyrios grabbed his wrist and flipped him onto his back before stomping his chest with a booted foot. All the wind was knocked out of Kyle and he wheezed uncontrollably. "Hauf! Ugh!"

"You are nothing, Kyle. Just a failed experiment and an embarrassment."

Kyrios began throttling him.

Kyle was losing. Kyle was going to die. Those thoughts raced through Chloe's head. She had dragged him into this with her cowardice, and now his life would end for the same reason.

No! She had to do something. But Kyrios' Satanic Gift prevented her from attacking him.

She was ashamed that moment. Kyrios' power had always been her fear of him. There was nothing physically stopping her from attacking him. Just the fear.

But Kyle had overcome that fear. She knew she had to do the same no matter what it took. Her hands trembled, but she managed to summon an electric knife. She couldn't hold it straight, though. It would surely miss if she threw it.

Through a Herculean effort, she managed to calm her breathing, but she remained terrified. She thought of Kyle and then it hit her; she wanted him to stay with her forever. And that could only happen if they stopped Kyrios.

She focused resolutely on the enemy, her terror beyond belief.

Kyle struggled against Kyrios' robot-like grip. Somehow, it was even stronger than Amelie's. However, he managed to pry Kyrios' left hand off him with his artificial one before punching the madman in the forehead. Kyrios groaned angrily but returned his hands to Kyle's throat.

Darkness crept in on Kyle. His eyes unconsciously drifted back to Chloe. Strangely, she seemed even more illuminated than usual.

The illumination shot towards them with lightning speed. It went over him and hit Kyrios in the chest. Kyrios cried out in rage and took his hands off Kyle's throat. Within moments, Kyle's vision cleared.

He got up to find Kyrios staggered with a burning hole in his chest. Though it had missed his heart, Kyle knew this was the only chance they would likely get. He scoured the ground for Kyrios' knife and seized it with his right hand. He lunged at Kyrios, intent on driving the knife deep into his chest.

Kyrios grabbed the wrist holding the knife and they stood locked in a stalemate. Kyle's metal hand had Kyrios' in a death grip. "This wound will heal in a few moments, Kyle. When it does, you die."

Kyle grunted with the exertion needed to overcome his enemy. "Better make it quick, then."

He focused all the strength he could into his metal hand and roared. Kyrios' was crushed in his. The madman shrieked but did not let go of the wrist holding the knife. "Don't think that will stop me, Kyle!" His voice was as venomous as any snake.

"No," Kyle said. "But this will." He opened his hand to drop the knife and his artificial hand grabbed it. He hammered it into Kyrios' chest like a railroad spike with strength and speed his organic appendage couldn't have achieved.

Kyrios' eyes widened in shock and he fell to his knees. Blood spurted from his mouth.

Kyle, equally wild-eyed, stared at him and desperately hoped this was the end. Strangely, his enemy now had a look of serenity on his face. His muscles were relaxed and his eyes normal. "Well done, Kyle."

And then there was nothing in Kyrios' eyes, just a blank emptiness. He remained prostrate even though Kyle had let go already.

"Good... aim," Chloe said. "Again." She had come over to help him. She visibly struggled with labored breathing and shaking legs. Whatever it had taken for her to overcome Kyrios' Gift had taken its toll on her physically.

Then, it was over. Kyle burst out laughing maniacally. He couldn't believe they had won. But they had.

They went back into the other room and untied the Grand Imam who shrank from them.

"Who are you?" he said, fear still etched into his features.

"Friends," Kyle said.

"You came to rescue me?" He looked horribly unsure of the whole situation.

"Yes," Chloe said.

They each took hold of him and helped him to his feet. Under the circumstances, he had no choice but to let them. He couldn't walk without assistance due to the injury from the APC.

"Kyle!" Jazmine cried out from somewhere on that floor.

"In here!" he called back.

Jazmine, Mel, and Shaun entered the room. They were all dirty as hell but apparently none the worse for wear. Shaun in particular was covered in dust and grime and had a weird green tint to him.

"Is it over?" Shaun said.

"That depends," Kyle said. "What about the other manzil members?

"Shaun killed one of them and me and Jaz sent the others flying off into the night. Cortez definitely got crushed."

"Let's hope that's enough," Kyle said.

They escorted Rabbani gingerly down the stairs and out into the night. No vampires attacked them, so Kyle dared to hope it was truly over.

No such luck. At that moment, Kyle sensed danger. He shoved the Grand Imam out of the way just as something hard slammed into his shoulder and propelled him into the side of the building. He hit the ground face first, inadvertently inhaling dirt. Chunks of brick rained down on his still-wet head.

* * *

A gunshot echoed and Kyle went down. Hurrying, Chloe used her superior hearing to locate the source of the attack. She spotted a lone Caucasian gunman in a black ops-looking outfit about fifty meters away to the south in some tall grass. She sped off after him in an erratic arc to throw off his aim.

He tossed an object which looked like a skinny Thermos bottle toward her. It abruptly exploded in a blinding flash of light and a deafening bang. Her senses were overwhelmed; she raised her arms to shield her eyes before pivoting to protecting her ears.

Devil's Intuition activated and she knew she had to drop to the ground, so she did. She sensed something flying over where she had been standing—probably another bullet.

She got up and began running after him. Her vision was beginning to clear and she could make out his vague shape up ahead. He ducked behind a small one-story brick building. She kept after him, albeit slower now due to caution. She didn't know how many more tricks he had up his sleeve.

She stuck her head behind the side of the building he had disappeared to. There was no sign of him. She would have been able to hear him except her hearing was still shot and might be for a while. Her only audible company was a powerful ringing.

Fortunately, her eyes were much better. A dark movement in the window, undetectable by mortals, alerted her and she executed a roll across the ground. A muzzle flash erupted inside the building and skewered the spot where she had been standing with bullets. Whoever this guy was, he was much more effective than the respective Grand Imam and Jericho's security forces.

Chloe crept by the corner of the building, making sure she was out of her enemy's line of sight. However, a small, round object flew out of the window. It landed on the ground near her and she recognized it as a grenade. She rounded the corner just in time to escape the blast. A decent chunk of the wall crumbled where she had been.

Time for a change of tactics. She began walking across the length of the building and striking the brick wall with the palms of her hands. The accosted bricks shot inward like mortars. She did this until she came to the other end. She estimated she had sent dozens of bricks rocketing into the room where the assailant was.

Chloe peered in the window and saw his fallen form on the ground. She swooped in and disarmed him before dragging him to his feet. He tried to run away but she caught him and wrestled the gun out of his hand. "Let me go!" he shouted in a French accent. Nothing doing.

She dragged him back to the group. Rabbani's eyes went wide again when he saw the assailant. "That's Le Faucon, the deadly assassin!"

Kyle had gotten back to his feet. "Why were you trying to kill the Grand Imam?"

"I'm not telling you anything!" He appeared to be middle-aged with strands of greying hair.

"Oh, yeah? Well, I'm getting hungry after everything we just went through." He ripped Faucon's tactical vest and shirt, exposing his shoulder. He then put his hands on said shoulder and began draining him. "You tell me when you feel like talking."

The assassin struggled against Kyle's preternatural strength but gave up as his blood level diminished. "All right! All right! The Russian paid me to kill the Grand Imam!"

"Mikhail?" Chloe said.

"I never got his name. He just said he wanted the target dead with nothing being traceable back to him."

Kyle removed his hand. "Mikhail had a Plan B."

Chloe punched Cain and knocked him out cold. He wouldn't wake up any time soon. In all likelihood, he would require hospitalization.

The distinctive *thumping* of helicopters sounded in the distance. "Looks like they found us," Mel said.

"They probably traced the signal from Kyrios' feed," Jazmine said.

"All right," Kyle said. "Let's get out of here." He turned to Rabbani. "Will you remember that we saved you? We don't want a holy war."

The Grand Imam was shaken but firm. "Yes. I will speak to Yousef Al-Bakir and ensure he does nothing drastic. Ealim al'Ahlam will not start a war because of this. Thank you. I thought all Americans were pigs, but you proved me wrong this night."

And with that, they departed before law enforcement arrived.

December 14.

The next night, they hung out at the bar and watched news coverage of recent events. "Authorities are still searching for the mysterious group that rescued the Grand Imam. They have a lot of questions to answer about what happened and who the other attackers were. Yousef Al-Bakir has gone on record saying the world only avoided a holy war because of the heroic actions of the unknown five people and that next time he would not be so forgiving."

"I call that a win," Jazmine said while serving bloody drinks behind the bar.

"Hell of a past two weeks, though," Mel added. "It was kind of fun. I mean, not for everyone. What was my point again?"

"The world is saved!" a partially-sloshed Kyle declared.

"Indeed, it is," came a deep voice behind him. He turned around. A large, scary-looking man stood mere inches from him. His first thought was that a previously unknown manzil member had come for revenge. He prepped his brain to be ready to act.

"Well, well. If it isn't Ducane," Mel said.

"Who?" Kyle asked.

Ducane said, "I'm a senior member of the Guide."

"Most nightwalkers know Ducane," Jazmine said. "He's the Guide's unofficial enforcer."

"What do you want with us?" Kyle said.

Ducane explained, "We saw you five on Kyrios' livestream last night. You prevented an apocalypse at great risk to yourselves. We want to show our gratitude by welcoming you into Dunia. You are hereby authorized to form your own manzil." He placed a thin stack of papers on the bar top. "Fill these out, and I'll be back later to collect them." He then left.

232

"Our own manzil," Shaun said.

"Well, this is an interesting turn of events," Kyle said.

Jazmine said, "Every manzil has a leader. Who will ours be?"

Kyle already knew the answer. "Nobody. We'll all be equals. Totally democratic. We'll be the Greenwich Street manzil."

"Nice," Chloe said.

"I don't live on Greenwich Street, but what the hell," Shaun said.

Jazmine poured herself a drink and raised her glass. "To the Greenwich Street manzil!"

"The Greenwich Street manzil!" They clinked their glasses together to cement their newfound status.

"Sour Cream's got a lot more training to do," Jazmine said. "He still doesn't have his Gift. Who wants to bet on how long it takes him to get it?"

Everyone did.

Epilogue

The previous night.

This person was in her room glued to the TV watching Kyrios' broadcast with horror. Angelica had been right, and they hadn't believed her. They should have sent everyone to guard the Grand Imam, but they hadn't and now it looked like there would be catastrophic consequences for their inaction.

"Kyrios!" someone said off-camera. She knew that voice but didn't believe it could truly be him.

"Ah. You have arrived. You are just in time."

"You're damn right I am! You're not doing this!"

No. It was impossible.

The mysterious figure charged Kyrios and they fought for a bit before a mysterious blue light hit the madman. The other guy emerged from the other room and she instantly recognized him.

"Kyle! You're alive!"

They had kept this from her. She seethed as she thought about what she would do to them because of this.

If you enjoyed the book, please leave a review.

Also, sign up for my mailing list to get exclusive content and news/reveals before anyone else, along with my 22-page tip guide for indie authors, as well as bonus stories set in my universes. Oh, and maybe a giveaway or two?

www.authorscottkinkade.com

Also by Scott Kinkade

The Game Called Revolution (Infini Calendar #1)

The French Revolution was never like this. Join Jeanne de Fleur and the knights of the Ordre as they sail the skies in their airship, the *Minuit Solaire*, battling to save France from a conspiracy that threatens all of Europe.

Published February 25, 2012

Science Fiction/Steampunk

236

God School (Divine Protector #1)

18-year-old Ev Bannen was just hoping to get admitted to college. He never expected to be recruited to a school for gods, where he'll be spending his days building up his strength, learning to answer prayers, and getting an education in religion alongside aspiring god of money Jaysin Marx, the lovely but troubled Maya Brünhart, and anger-prone ginger Daryn Anders.

But when the world is threatened, Ev must step up to save the day.

Published December 9, 2014.

Urban fantasy

About the author

Scott Kinkade lives in Oklahoma where he struggles to put words to paper. He graduated from Oklahoma Christian University with a BA in Arts. His major was English/Writing. He enjoys reading, writing, TV, anime, video games, and comic books/manga. He has an unhealthy interest in history which is sure to get him in trouble one day.

Scott provides proofreading services at www.authorscottkinkade.com. You can also follow him on Twitter @SK_Author, and Instagram @scottkinkadestravels.

www.ingramcontent.com/pod-product-compliance
Lightning Source LLC
Chambersburg PA
CBHW070525100726
47907CB00004B/987